THE DUMPSTER

One Woman's Search for Love

By

Becky Due

TELEMACHUS PRESS

This book is a work of fiction. Names, characters, places and incidents are either the product of the author's imagination or are used fictitiously. Any resemblance to actual persons, living or dead, or to actual events or locales is entirely coincidental.

The Dumpster

The publisher does not have any control over and does not assume any responsibility for author or third-party websites or their content.

Cover Designed by Book Masters, Inc.

Published by Telemachus Press, LLC
http://www.telemachuspress.com

Visit the author website:
http://www.BeckyDue.com

Library of Congress Control Number: 2012948304

ISBN # 978-1-938701-44-3 (eBook)
ISBN # 978-1-938701-45-0 (Paperback)

Version 2012.09.11

Printed in the United States of America

10 9 8 7 6 5 4 3 2 1

A Light-Hearted Romantic Comedy for All Women

THE

DUMPSTER

One Woman's Search for Love

Chapter 1

NICOLE WAS FRANTICALLY getting ready for her Valentine's party. Her condo was perfectly decorated with hearts and streamers in red, pink and white. Her living room was rearranged to accommodate all her friends, and her kitchen was set up with an area for drinks and an area for the snacks. She hoped all the guests would B.Y.O.B. because she didn't have a lot of booze. She had plenty of beer and a few bottles of the hard stuff: vodka, tequila and gin.

Nicole finished applying her makeup and headed to the closet to get dressed. She hurried into the little black dress she had purchased for the special night, then stepped in front of the full-length mirror. "Ugh," she groaned, sucking in her tummy and wondering why she always had to be the chunky one with a cute face. And she was cute. She had long natural-blond hair, pretty blue eyes and nice skin, but she was overweight by twenty pounds, sometimes thirty pounds. She couldn't remember a time when she hadn't been a little chubby.

Nicole walked over to the bed, fluffed the pillows and sprayed a little perfume across her comforter. She was looking forward to a romantic evening with her boyfriend, Tom, once the party was over. The setting in her bedroom was perfect for passion. She had bought red satin sheets and a small heart-shaped pillow for the bed. Champagne was hidden in the refrigerator and a sexy red negligee hung in her closet. Candles were everywhere, and she had a CD of love songs to play in the background while they made love. Too much of their love making had just felt like sex, so her plan tonight was to slow things down and make love.

This Valentine's night would be a romantic night to remember. Nicole's fantasy was that Tom would propose to her on a Valentine's Day, and they would marry on a Valentine's Day, and it would be all because of this night she had made special, the night he realized how much he loved her.

"Hello, Nicole! The place looks great!"

Nicole rushed out of her bedroom and greeted Roxanne with a hug. "You look beautiful."

Roxanne was petite with brown hair and beautiful brown eyes, though she often hid her eyes behind long bangs. She was little in so many ways; even her personality was not the most memorable. But the one thing about Roxanne that all women liked was that she was always on your side, the side of the woman. If Nicole needed a pity party, she called Roxanne. Roxanne believed in love more than anything, and she was patiently waiting for Mr. Right to knock on her door.

"I can't wait to meet Tom."

Nicole grabbed her by the hand. "You have to see this." She led her into her bedroom.

"Oh, my goodness, this is beautiful." Roxanne started to cry. "I'm so happy for you. I wish I could find a good man."

"Oh, you're next; I can feel it." They hugged, and then heard Renee come in. "We're in the bedroom," Nicole hollered.

"Where do you want me to put this stuff?" Renee yelled back.

Nicole and Roxanne headed to the kitchen to help her unload her booze and snacks.

Renee was tall, thin and stunning, with a dark complexion and hair that changed color and style every week. Renee's career was in what she called hair artistry or hair design. She was certainly not something so ordinary as a beautician or hair stylist—she was an artist. Renee was famous in the city, and she did only the richest and most famous people's hair. She was in the midst of parlaying her incredible career into marketing a new product line and fragrance that would move her career beyond just the local scene. Renee was happily married to a mechanic, whose business expanded in his wife's wake as he became the mechanic to all of Renee's clients. Renee and Jason were money smart and incredibly in love.

Nicole had once read in *Cosmo* that the best female lovers were hair stylists and the best male lovers were mechanics. When she saw Renee and Jason together, that's what she always thought of. What luck to have found each other.

"Oh, Nicole, you did a great job decorating. It's perfect."

"Thanks. Where's Jason?"

"Oh, you know him; he'll stop by later for a bit. I'm sure he won't stay long, just long enough to check on me and tell me to stay out of trouble."

"But it's Valentine's Day."

"Yeah. He's not into it."

Both Nicole and Roxanne looked at her sadly.

"Knock it off you guys, I'd rather be with you anyway." She gave Nicole a nudge. "Besides, you wait until you get married, you'll figure it out. That kind of thing isn't important. In my opinion, I have Valentine's Day everyday because I have a man who adores me."

Nicole and Roxanne's look changed from sadness to envy.

Cheering up, Nicole said, "Well, I found my special love. I can't wait for you guys to meet him. You'll love him."

The doorbell rang and the party began

Chapter 2

ABOUT AN HOUR later, Nicole checked her home phone and cell phone messages. Nobody had called. She was beginning to get worried about Tom, and it didn't help that everybody kept asking her where he was. "He's running late, but he'll be here."

Nicole found herself drinking a little more than she should and knew she must slow down. Pulling Renee aside, she said, "Don't let me drink anymore. He's not here…"

"I know, Nicky, but don't worry, he'll come." She grabbed the beer out of Nicole's hand and handed her a bottle of water.

"Thank you. I love you. I really love you," Nicole said and started to cry.

"Oh, my God! How much have you been drinking?"

"I don't know."

Renee led her into her bedroom, closed the door and went straight to the window to open it. "You need some fresh air."

Just as she said that, Nicole yelled, "No, don't!" But it was too late. The smell filled her bedroom.

"What is that?" Renee asked, closing the window.

"They moved that dumpster below my bedroom window."

"That's disgusting!"

"I know. I've complained several times to the manager, who I call Rick the Dick. He hates me. The smell isn't always that bad, but it's bad tonight."

"Nicky, that's awful! They need to get that moved right away."

"I don't care about that... Where is he?"

"Did you tell him that the party started at nine and that he was going to meet your friends?"

"Yes, I told him."

"How did he sound when you told him?"

"Excited… I think."

"Well, okay then, he'll be here. In fact, he's probably out there right now looking for you." She helped Nicole up from the bed. "Your bedroom looks sexy and romantic… don't drink anymore."

"I know. I won't," Nicole said, and the two of them rejoined the party.

About an hour later, Tom showed up. He didn't look happy and wasn't pleasant to her friends. Impatiently, he rushed her into the bedroom saying, "I need to talk to you in private."

Nicole smiled broadly as they walked into her bedroom. She said, "Before you say anything, this was supposed to be a surprise, but I'll give you a sneak peak." She turned on the stereo with the remote control. Michael Bolton's "When a Man Loves a Woman" started playing. "This is for us for after the party," she said as seductively as she could manage and turned toward him for the expected hug and kiss. But he put his hands up to hold her back.

"What?"

Tom shook his head and said softly, "I didn't want any of this." He exhaled loudly. "I was afraid of this." He reached under his trench coat and pulled out a DVD player.

"Oh, my God, you got me a Valentine's present. I didn't get you anything… well, but this party is for you… and our private party after the party." She smiled as she took his gift.

"I have to go. There's a DVD in this. Watch it," he said, and left the room.

"But we're going to make love tonight… I have a sexy nighty…"

Nicole sat there confused looking at the DVD player. Roxanne and Renee rushed in.

"He had to go." Nicole said in confusion. "But he gave me this for Valentine's Day."

"What the hell's going on?" Renee asked.

"I don't know. He said there was a DVD inside and I'm supposed to watch it."

The three of them sat on the bed and watched the DVD while the Valentine's party for her boyfriend was raging on without him and without her. "Nicole, I think you are a sweet girl."

"Oh, oh!" Renee said under her breath as they watched the talking head.

"I'm just going to say it: I used you. You were easy, very easy. You did what I wanted when I wanted. You gave me sex whenever I wanted it. I didn't want a relationship, and I thought you knew that. But then you mentioned this party. You're cute, but you're not my type. Don't call me crying because I don't want to talk to you again. Have a nice life." The screen went blue.

Renee handed Nicole her beer, grabbed the DVD player, opened the window and threw it into the dumpster. Roxanne and Nicole stood up and looked out the window.

"Pee-u! Why do you have a dumpster out there?" Roxanne asked Nicole.

"I don't know," she said, wanting to cry.

Renee closed the window. "How long were you and Tom together?"

"I don't know, about two weeks."

Renee burst out laughing. "Two weeks? Nicky! You made it sound like you were a serious couple!"

"We were."

"You spent almost every night together, right? Two weeks is a long time," Roxanne said, defending Nicole, and scolding Renee.

"Oh, my God!" Renee grabbed her beer back from Nicole and chugged it. "Let me guess. He's a player, isn't he?"

"Well, I mean, I heard things at the bank, but I thought I…"

"You thought you could change him. Oh, Nicky!" She took Roxanne's beer and handed it to Nicole. "Come on! Let's go party!"

"Renee, you threw out a perfectly good DVD player."

"Trust me, you don't want anything that man gave you. Besides, he's the biggest geek I've ever heard of. Who breaks up with somebody via DVD?"

Nicole was depressed during the rest of the party and didn't tell anybody the truth about why he didn't stay or for those who came later, why he didn't show up. Her stories became more elaborate the more inebriated she became.

"He's a doctor and he was on call, emergency surgery."

"He's in the Special Forces Marines and he was called to duty. I shouldn't even be telling you this."

"He's a pilot for a billionaire and had to fly the billionaire and his wife to Paris for a romantic Valentine's Day." She hoped nobody would figure out the Paris time difference.

"He's a sports reporter and there was some big news with Shaquille O'Neal, so he had to go and cover the story. You'll read all about it in the newspaper tomorrow."

As the party wound down, Nicole, Roxanne and Renee seemed to get a second wind. They cranked up '90s tunes on the stereo and sang and danced while they cleaned up. Nicole opened her bedroom window and the three of them threw out the Styrofoam cups and paper plates. They tossed out the empty bottles, trying to make as much noise as possible. They popped the balloons and tore down the streamers. Everything went out the window and into the dumpster.

When they settled down, Nicole became sad again. "My boyfriend broke up with me on Valentine's Day. I was dumped on Valentine's Day."

"Nicky, I don't think he was your boyfriend," Renee said, rolling her eyes.

"Shut up! He was, too!" Roxanne snapped and gave Nicole a hug.

"I have an idea!" Renee exclaimed. "You know how he said you made everything easy for him? You know how he called you easy?"

"Yes, I saw the DVD. I was there," Nicole answered sarcastically.

Renee scooted in next to Nicole. "Maybe you should stop being so easy. Let's make him remember you as being not easy at all."

"What do you mean?"

"Let's go find his car and put a screwdriver in his tires!"

Nicole started laughing. "Okay, let's do it!"

Roxanne hesitated.

Renee called her husband. "Jason, if I get into trouble tonight, will you bail me out of jail? Okay, thanks, honey. I'll see you later. Love you. Bye."

They looked in Nicole's junk drawer for a screwdriver. They found only the kind with a flat end but figured it would work just fine. Roxanne had drunk the least that night, so she drove to Tom's apartment. They had their fingers crossed that he had parked outside and not in the garage. They searched the parking lot and spotted his BMW. Because it was close to three in the morning, nobody was around. They parked their car and walked toward Tom's car giggling and shushing each other as their high-heels clicked on the pavement.

"Where's the screwdriver?" Nicole whispered.

Nobody had it, so Roxanne ran back to the car to get it; then all three squatted down by Tom's BMW. Nicole held the screwdriver tightly in her fist with the flat end against the tire. "Will the tire blow up?"

"That's what I was wondering," Roxanne said quietly.

"No, it won't blow up."

"How do you know?"

"Just do it!"

Nicole lifted her arm and turned her head away in fear, noticing that Roxanne and Renee were also turned away. "Then why are you afraid? I saw you turning your head! It's going to blow up, isn't it?"

Roxanne decided to be brave and stand up for her friend. "Give it to me. I'll do it!" Renee and Nicole looked at each other impressed. She took the tool from Nicole, who was now sitting on the pavement leaning against the car.

She hit the tire with the screwdriver, but nothing happened. She hit the tire again. "Shit!" She looked at her fingers. "I broke my nail! I just got these done for the party. Damn it! Ouch! Look at this!"

Both Nicole and Renee took a good look. "Oh, that's awful! How far down did it go?"

"I don't know but it hurts!" She put her finger in her mouth.

"I did that just last week when I was helping Jason with some car, and oh, did it hurt!" She looked at her hand. "My manicurist got me in right away and she fixed it." She showed Roxanne her nails. "See, but I did go a little shorter. It's easier."

Renee grabbed the screwdriver from next to Roxanne and forcefully hit Tom's tire. Nothing happened. "Maybe these are special tires." She hit it again even harder, and again. Still nothing happened.

The three of them sat leaning against Tom's car sitting on the cool parking lot pavement in their new dresses, when Nicole said, "Happy Valentine's Day" and started laughing. Roxanne started laughing and farted loudly. The contagious laughter took over. They couldn't stop and before they knew what had happened, Renee had peed on the pavement, which only made them laugh harder.

Tom's tires were safe that night.

Chapter 3

WHEN NICOLE GOT home, she put on her red negligee, crawled into bed and fell asleep immediately. When she woke up, around five-thirty in the morning, still drunk, she felt an urgent need to get that DVD player and watch it again. She just didn't understand what he meant or why he dumped her. She grabbed her robe, slipped on her tennis shoes and headed to the back exit of her building. She walked down the one flight of fire-escape stairs to the dumpster in the alley.

Nicole took off her white robe. She didn't want to get it dirty, but she didn't care about her nighty. She hoisted herself up, kicked one leg over the dumpster side and sat on the edge looking for the DVD player. The smell was thick in the humid morning air. She kicked a bag of garbage and saw the player. She jumped in and grabbed it. The smell was making her gag. Garbage from the party was all around her: red streamers, popped balloons, unbroken bottles and paper plates. But it was other people's garbage that was making her queasy.

Suddenly, she thought of rats and she started panicking. She moaned as she held on to the DVD player and tried to figure out how to get out of the dumpster. The smell was suffocating her. She grabbed the filthy side of the bin and leaped to get out, but there was something greasy under her hand and she lost her grip as she tried to jump, falling back inside. She landed in smelly, nasty, wet garbage. "Oh, my God!" She stood up, then slipped again twisting her ankle and landing in something even more disgusting. She looked herself over to make sure she hadn't landed in broken glass. Luckily, they weren't able to break the bottles they had thrown in the night before even though they had tried.

Her panic increased as she pictured the garbage men emptying the bin with her inside. The big truck would lift the dumpster and empty everything into the compressor. She would be killed. Nicole started hyperventilating. She stood up again and was suddenly face to face with a man. She was so startled she fell back down again.

"You don't look like a piece of garbage to me," her visitor said.

"Can you help me? I accidently threw something away, but I found it," she said, holding up the DVD player. "But now I can't get out." Before she knew it, he was in the dumpster with her. He looked her up and down as if she were the sexiest woman alive. She forgot she was in her Valentine's sex outfit. "Yes. I know! Just help me out of here."

He cupped his hands for her to step in. She put one foot on his folded hands, but before she was able to kick her leg over the dumpster, her foot fell through his hands and they both fell. He wasn't strong enough to lift her. She was humiliated.

"I'm sorry," he said. "I didn't have a good grip."

"It's fine. I'm heavier than I look."

"Well, you look good to me."

She exhaled, irritated. She found a box in the corner and started piling the cleaner garbage on top of it. She stepped up on the garbage and was high enough to work her way out. Her hero's hands on her ass pushing didn't help in the least.

Once she was out, he jumped out of the dumpster like a stray cat. She felt terrible that he got dirty because of her. "Thank you for your help," she said, and grabbed her robe but didn't cover up. "What were you doing in this alley?"

"Oh, my buddy owns that bar the next block over, and I couldn't find a place to park my bike last night," he said, pointing to his motorcycle.

She suddenly realized how good looking he was, so she tried to keep the conversation going. "His bar's still open?"

"Naw, we were just hanging out."

"Well, I better take a shower. I'm Nicole."

"Stan." His eyes were the most seductive eyes she had ever seen. Biting his bottom lip, he studied her with a playful grin as if he knew something she didn't.

***

After Nicole and Stan showered, they made love all afternoon on the red satin Valentine's sheets that she had bought for Tom. Nicole wasn't about to sit around and cry over some guy who broke up with her via DVD. No, she was not going to let one bad apple ruin the bunch. Everything must happen for a reason, she thought, because Tom's breakup had led to her meeting Stan.

She had never dated anybody like Stan. He had a lot of tattoos and he rode a motorcycle, usually not her type, but maybe she had overlooked a portion of the population that wasn't so bad. She decided to keep an open mind and see where this new relationship would take her.

Nicole and Stan exchanged phone numbers before he left, and he asked her if he could come over that night when he got off work. Not caring what he did or why he worked on Saturday, she agreed and was excited that he was interested in her. She couldn't believe it—she already had a new boyfriend. She couldn't wait to call Roxanne and Renee to share her great news. But she called Blaine and Christian instead.

Christian and his partner, Blaine, were the loves of Nicole's life. Christian was an interior decorator and designer, and Blaine was a very successful real estate agent. They were, well, Christian was the most honest friend she had ever had when it came to her looks; Blaine was a little less blunt. They met at an AIDS walk about eight years earlier when Nicole was the heaviest she had ever been. She had gained more than her college fifteen and decided to start walking to lose the weight. She signed up for the AIDS walk with a group of friends from school who were also walking to lose weight.

Nicole overheard Christian telling Blaine that, "Blondie would be cute if she'd drop fifty pounds."

"Fifty? Are you kidding me?" Nicole mouthed off.

They had been the best of friends ever since. Nicole depended on them for more than friendship; they had become her decorators and her entertaining personal stylists, too.

"Guurl, you better get right back in there and change. You are not wearing that out with me."

"Oh, no, honey! Your makeup is all wrong."

"Oh, Nicole, who did that to you? Your friend Renee better make some time for you to fix that hair."

"Where did you get that blouse? It's fabulous!"

"Guurl, you better step on that scale. You're letting it get away from you again."

They told her when to get a manicure, pedicure and facial. They convinced her to get laser hair removal under her arms and her bikini line. They helped her with decorating her condo. They even helped her judge boyfriends. So she called them to tell them all about her luck in finding a new boyfriend so quickly. They weren't back from their vacation in Paris yet, so she just left a long, detailed message on their voicemail.

When she heard a loud motorcycle pull into the alley later that night, she was excited and eager to see Stan again. Standing at the door, he had the same seductive look on his face. His eyes caressed her. She loved his teeth and his lips and his eyes and the way he used them. He was incredibly sexy. They started making out the second the door was closed.

Early the next morning after the third time they made love, Nicole was about to take the condom to the bathroom to flush it. But she couldn't find it. It wasn't on his penis like it had been every other time.

"Where's the condom?"

"Right here," he said, reaching for his penis and shrugging when he couldn't find the condom either. "I don't know. Come here." He held his arms out to her.

"Did you wear a condom?"

"Of course."

"Then where is it?" she said as she started lifting the covers. She felt all around the bed and couldn't find it. She got up out of bed and turned on the light. She frantically searched for the used condom. "Where is it?" she cried. But he didn't seem to care, just lying there still, half asleep.

She stormed out of the room and went to the bathroom. Before she sat on the toilet, she reached between her legs to feel if it was hanging out of her. She felt nothing. Then she stuck her finger inside to see if she could feel anything. At first she was a little surprised by the way she felt, warm and squishy. "Huh, so that's what it feels like." But then she felt something. It was the edge of the condom. She curled the tip of her finger to get a grip on the condom and she slowly pulled it out.

"Oh, thank God," she breathed, but her elation quickly evaporated as she thought of getting pregnant or a disease. She held the condom up to the light, and saw that is was full of sperm. "Okay, it must have still been on him when he came," she said, still wondering if any of it had seeped out of the condom.

She dropped it into the toilet, then sat down and peed quickly. She went back to the bedroom and asked, "Stan, do you have any sexually transmitted diseases?"

"What? No. No way!" He was suddenly wide awake. "Do you?"

"Uh! No, of course not!" She was pissed he even asked such a thing.

"I always use a condom."

"So do I."

"I used a condom with Trish earlier. And I'll use a condom with Mary tomorrow night."

Nicole's eyes went wide and she felt the room spinning. "What! You had sex with another woman… yesterday!"

"But I saved the best for last. Come here," he said reaching for her. "Come back to bed."

"You have to leave now!" she said, frantically gathering his clothes. "Get dressed! You're leaving!"

He was half dressed as she pushed him out the door.

She ran to her bedroom with angry tears running down her cheeks, and stripped her bed. She opened the bedroom window and tossed her new satin sheets into the dumpster. She ran to the bathroom sink where she was soaking her little red negligee and carried that dripping to the window and threw it out. The romantic CD with "When a Man Loves a Woman" went straight out the window, with the heart-shaped pillow following.

Feeling dirty and scared, she jumped in the shower and scrubbed her body. She got dressed, put her hair in a ponytail and headed straight to the grocery store.

At the store, she grabbed four things: a gallon of milk, a tube of readymade chocolate-chip cookie dough, a douche and a pregnancy test. She looked at the checkout lines, choosing the one with only a young woman waiting. The woman was tall, thin and tan, and was wearing a white tank top over a red bra or swimsuit top. Her cellulite-free legs were perfect in her not-too-short cutoff jean shorts. Her sandy blonde hair was pulled back in a low pony tail with her sunglasses resting on top of her head. She was perfect.

Nicole didn't want to stand next to her, or behind her. She turned toward a longer line, but her left flip-flop stuck to the floor and she tripped, dropping her douche. "Oh, my God!" She bent over to pick it up, and dropped her cookie dough.

The perfect woman hurried over. "Here, let me help you," she said, glancing at the pregnancy test and cookie dough before giving Nicole a pitying look.

Nicole was mortified. "This is my typical Sunday shopping spree," she said sarcastically. "I change it up a little... sometimes I get the floral-scented douche or I'll get the M&M cookie dough." She quickly moved toward the longer checkout line.

"Hey, aren't you a friend of Renee's? She does my hair."

"Oh, my God. Yes." She walked back to the perfect woman. "I'm sorry, I'm just... humiliated right now."

"I'm Joy. I had a rough weekend, too." She turned so Nicole could see inside the basket she was carrying. She had a box of large condoms, a dozen powdered sugar donuts and a two-liter bottle of Diet Mountain Dew.

"It couldn't be that bad," Nicole said, tapping the box of condoms.

"My small-penised boyfriend dumped me two weeks ago. I guess he didn't want to have to deal with Valentine's Day. So, in fact, it was Renee who suggested I buy a box of large condoms. She said, 'If you build it, they will come'." Joy started laughing after hearing herself sound so ridiculous.

Nicole burst out laughing. "That's the dumbest thing I ever heard!"

"You're right, it is," Joy agreed, and reached into her basket and set the box of condoms on the shelf by the tabloid magazines.

With a straight face, Nicole casually picked up the box and added it to her basket of goodies.

The cashier was waiting for Joy to put her items on the conveyor, but Joy was bent over laughing. She stepped aside to let Nicole pay for her things, including the box of condoms. Joy turned and ran with her hand between her legs to the bathroom by the pharmacy, and to get herself a new box of large condoms.

Nicole waited for Joy, and the two of them went for coffee at the Starbucks nearby. They were immediate friends. Joy thought Nicole was the funniest person she had ever met, and Nicole was still in shock that somebody so beautiful and kind could have man problems. Nicole loved to watch Joy's profile while she spoke. Her nose was the cutest thing she had ever seen; when she talked, the tip of her nose bend toward her mouth. Nicole was mesmerized by her, and it didn't even matter what she said. After sharing their man troubles over a couple vanilla lattes, they exchanged phone numbers and email addresses, promising to keep each other posted on their "field of dreams."

When Nicole got home, she put her now warm milk and cookie dough in the freezer, and her condoms and pregnancy test in the bedroom. Then she went into the bathroom to douche.

Though having coffee and laughing with Joy had lightened her mood, everything rushed back to her as soon as she was back in her condo, and it wasn't funny. She still had to worry about disease and pregnancy. She made her bed on the couch, turned on the TV and flipped through the channels until she found Lifetime. Then she went to the kitchen to get a big glass of milk with ice cubes and the cookie dough before settling in to watch TV.

Nicole became immersed in the Lifetime movie about a woman trying to find out who murdered her best friend. She ate cookie dough and drank iced milk, and forgot about her own problems. An hour later, Nicole was fast asleep on the couch.

She woke with the same dread of disease and pregnancy, only now she was annoyed that she had fallen asleep and didn't know how the movie ended. Another movie had already started, something to do with a baby mix up at the hospital, but she didn't want to get interested in it. Nicole flipped through the channels and decided to watch Headline News. She reached next to her on the end table for her cookie dough and started spooning it in. The dough was much softer now and warm, but it was hitting the spot.

She was depressed. She wanted to turn the clock back to Valentine's Day when everything was fine. She wanted everything that happened after Valentine's Day morning to be a bad dream. She was not looking forward to work the next day, and she didn't want to talk to Roxanne or Renee. She thought about calling in sick or taking a personal day, but she knew she would need to use that day off to go to the doctor and get tested for STDs.

Something on the news caught Nicole's attention. She took another spoonful of cookie dough and closed her eyes, savoring her favorite treat. Turning the volume up on her TV, she heard, "Raw cookie dough is the latest source of this recent E-coli outbreak." Nicole took a deep breath. "Well..." and turned off the TV. "That's about right." Her stomach started hurting immediately at the thought of E-coli poisoning. She got up and walked into the bedroom, opened the window and threw the cookie dough and spoon into the dumpster. She closed the window, crawled into her freshly made bed, set her alarm and went to sleep.

Chapter 4

THE FOLLOWING WEDNESDAY evening Nicole was sitting in the waiting room at Planned Parenthood for her six-thirty appointment. She was a month early for her yearly physical, but she needed to be tested for all STDs and pregnancy. Nicole was grateful that she didn't have to take time off from work. Renee called her while she was waiting.

"I shouldn't talk right now; I'm at Planned Parenthood."

"Why?" Renee asked.

"I didn't want to tell you, but I met somebody after our party. He was really nice and well… we fooled around."

"What do you mean?" Renee laughed.

"Well, I don't know, maybe I needed a distraction from being hurt by Tom. I guess it was a fling. So now that's over and I need to be checked."

"Didn't you use a condom?"

"Yes, but it slipped off and now I'm scared because I guess he sleeps with a lot of women."

"Nicky, do you want me to come and wait with you?"

"No, I'm sure they'll call me any minute."

"Well, when you are finished, call me. I want to hear all about this rebound guy."

"Oh, trust me, you don't."

Renee started laughing.

Nicole took a deep breath, then exhaled. "Renee, we met in the dumpster."

"What?" She roared with laughter.

"Yes. I wanted to get that DVD player… It's a long story."

Renee's laughter made Nicole laugh.

"They're ready for me. I gotta go. I'll talk to you soon."

"Let's have dinner when you're done. Call me."

Nicole followed the nurse into the examining room. Sitting on the table in a paper gown, Nicole thought about her sexual behavior. She read the poster that she had read every other time she was in Planned Parenthood: that she had slept with every person every person she slept with slept with. She didn't want to be one of those people who had sex with anybody any time. She wanted a relationship and love. She wasn't okay with sexual freedom because it didn't make her feel free; it made her feel trapped, worried and unhappy.

The doctor came in and they briefly went over the reasons Nicole was there and discussed the importance of protection, especially if she wasn't in a relationship. Nicole lay down on the table.

"I need you to scoot down a little further and drop your knees open," the doctor said as she put on her latex gloves.

Nicole did as she was told.

"Okay now this is going to be a little uncomfortable."

Nicole didn't mind getting a pap smear. It never seemed to bother her the way it did others.

"Wow, you have a beautiful cervix! In fact, you have the prettiest cervix I've ever seen."

"Really?"

"Hasn't anybody ever told you that your cervix is perfect?"

"No."

"Well, it is. It's textbook." Then she asked, "Have you ever seen your cervix?"

"No, I haven't."

"Would you like to?"

"Well… sure," Nicole said, wondering how they would pull that off.

The doctor told her to sit up a little, then held up a mirror. "How's this? Can you see it?"

"Is it that pink thing?"

"Yes. Isn't it beautiful?"

"Yes," Nicole agreed, but never would have used the word beautiful to describe her internal organs.

"Would you mind if I had one of my colleagues come in and take a look at your cervix?"

"No, that's fine."

Lying on the table alone, with her legs spread wide and her vagina wide open, she supposed she couldn't possibly be on Candid Camera.

By the time she left Planned Parenthood with her bag full of regular-sized condoms, three others had viewed her cervix. Nicole felt very pretty because of her cervix. She had never been the prettiest one in any situation, but her cervix was a ten. As good as she felt, she still had to wait for her test results. Her pregnancy test was negative, but it was too early to know for sure.

After her appointment and before she met Renee for dinner, Nicole stopped at the drugstore to buy some air freshener. Her dumpster was stinking more than ever, and she was hoping she could camouflage it with air freshener. She bought more vanilla air-freshener plug-ins and about four cans of spray: lavender, vanilla-sandalwood, ocean breeze and melon rush.

When she got to the restaurant, Roxanne was with Renee and they were anxious to hear about her rebound guy. But Nicole was more interested in telling them about her beautiful cervix.

"Nicole, do you think that maybe you should stop dating for a while?" Roxanne asked.

Renee laughed. "I don't think what she's doing is called dating."

"Rox, that wasn't planned. He was just so sexy. I mean the way he bit his lip while he looked at me seductively."

"You met him in an alley—in a dumpster."

"I know, I know." Nicole took a deep breath. "But I also felt guilty that he got so dirty helping me."

Renee interrupted, "I just want to know, are you sad about Tom? Do you think about Tom?"

"No."

"So there, you had a nice fast rebound. Good for you."

"I don't think about Tom or Stan. I only want to know that I'm not pregnant and haven't got a disease. That is all I can focus on right now."

"But Nicole, I think you should dig a little deeper and find out why it was so easy for you to jump in bed with another guy so quickly. I thought you really liked Tom."

"I guess you didn't hear me," Nicole said in a singsong voice. "Stan had this look in his eyes, and he bit his lip while looking at my body."

"That's not funny."

"I know. But… all right, Rox…" Nicole said in frustration. "Why is it that you haven't had a boyfriend for over two years? You haven't even been on a date. Why is that?"

"Here we go again," Renee cut in. "Live and let live. Okay?"

"Well, at least I'm out there trying to find somebody. At least I'm having fun."

"Oh, is that what that's called, Mrs. Planned Parenthood?"

Nicole thought for a minute. "Yeah, I am having fun. It sucks about the condom, but I sure had fun," she said, grinning mischievously.

Renee gave her a high five. "Good for you! I know what it is." She turned to Roxanne. "If a guy gives you a compliment, you become suspicious and you avoid him like the plague." She turned to Nicole. "And you, if a guy pays attention to you or says nice things to you, you start thinking about the possibilities and you open yourself up—literally."

"You're right. I get a compliment or special attention and I start thinking about our future together. And it doesn't even have to be from a guy," she giggled. "I mean, you wouldn't believe my thoughts about my cervix-loving doctor. We were going to buy a house together and spend our free time fighting for the right to marry. And she's already married… to a man."

All three of them started laughing.

"Nicole, you don't even realize how pretty you are and what a great personality you have," Roxanne said. "Some guy is going to be so happy and lucky to have you."

Nicole leaned over and gave her a quick hug. "Thank you, Rox. That means a lot to me."

Renee looked at Roxanne and said quietly, "Careful." She raised her eyebrows and nodded her head toward Nicole. "Or you two will be fighting for your right to marry."

Chapter 5

ON FRIDAY NIGHT, with nothing major planned for the weekend, Nicole had a surprise visit from her mother.

Nicole grew up in Minnesota, then moved with her mom and dad to Naples, Florida, when she was sixteen. After she graduated from high school, she went to college in Miami where she made tons of friends and established her career in banking. Even though Nicole loved Miami, she sometimes missed the simple life with her parents in Cannon Falls, Minnesota, when she was young. But she never wanted to move back to Cannon Falls or Naples because she liked the activity and nightlife of the big city. Miami was her home.

Her mother got right to the point. "Your father and I sensed that you were depressed after your party and what happened with this Tom fellow, so I decided to come to the city to cheer you up. Get dressed. We're going out for dinner."

"Mom, I wish you would've called," Nicole said, thinking of the things she would have taken to her storage closet in the parking garage before her parents visited: condoms, vibrator, pregnancy test, lingerie, bottles of booze. "Okay, Mom, get comfortable in the living room, and I'll go get dressed."

"Look nice because we're going to find you a good man tonight."

"Mom!" Nicole's face twisted in frustration as she headed to the bedroom and heard her mom laughing.

"Honey, do you have anything to drink?"

Nicole decided not to worry about the alcohol, because she had just had a party. "Yeah, there's some pop or bottles of water in the fridge." Nicole was thankful that the pregnancy test, condoms, vibrator and lingerie were all in her bedroom. She stuffed them all into her overnight bag and threw it up on the top shelf in the closet. She quickly put on the same clothes she had worn to work. She glanced in the mirror, fluffed her hair and walked into the living room. "Okay, I'm ready."

Her mom walked out of the kitchen with a glass of Coke and was pouring in some whisky. "I hope you don't mind. It was a long drive here, and I need to unwind."

"No, that's fine. Help yourself." Nicole was a little surprised. "How's Daddy?"

"He's great. He misses you."

"Why didn't he come, too?"

"We both thought you may need some girl time."

Nicole had never heard her mom talk like that. Nicole's girl time was with her girlfriends, but she decided to give it a shot. She had also never seen her mother drink without her father around. "Okay, well, should we go?"

"Sure." She chugged her drink and took the glass to the kitchen. As she walked out of the kitchen, she unbuttoned the top two buttons of her blouse. "How does this look? Sexy?"

"Mom, you're married. You don't have to be sexy."

"Oh, honey, you always have to be sexy."

"Mom, are you okay? Maybe we should stay in tonight."

"Everything is fine. Call up your friends and let's have a party. Or only invite the boys so I can pick one for you."

"Mom, I don't need help and I don't need a boyfriend." Now she was starting to sound like Roxanne. "Mom, did you drink before you got here?"

"Just a little."

"Oh, Mom, is something wrong? Is everything okay with you and Dad?" she asked in panic.

"Everything's fine. Maybe I just wanted to cut loose a little with my daughter. You're having so much fun here in Miami, and maybe I just wanted to have some fun, too."

"Well, okay then, let's have some fun." Nicole turned up the music, then went into the kitchen, grabbed a beer and made her mom another drink. Nicole changed into a going-out dancing skirt and blouse and added some makeup. She called Rox and Renee, and the two of them joined Nicole and her mom for a night on the town. On the way to the bar, Nicole's mom sat in front and flirted with the cab driver, making Nicole squirm in embarrassment. Roxanne and Renee kept squeezing Nicole's legs after every remark her mother made. Nicole could tell they were fighting hysterical laughter at her mother's behavior.

Nicole whispered to Roxanne, "Midlife crisis?" then turned and whispered the same to Renee.

Roxanne and Renee leaned forward as if comparing notes, then nodded. "Yep," they both said out loud.

"Yep what?" Mom asked.

"We all agree you look great tonight, Mom." Nicole wasn't lying; she did think her mother looked great. Nicole got her coloring and body type from her dad, unfortunately. Her mother was a beautiful middle-aged woman. She had short brown hair and beautiful eyes. She was slender and medium height. Her mother always dressed nicely and smelled wonderful; she had a thing for expensive perfume.

At the bar, her mother danced with every man who would dance with her. She wasn't picky. She danced with the men who were too old to be hanging out there, though they were younger than her mom. She danced with the regulars who hit on everybody. She danced with the young guys who were hoping she was a cougar. Nicole, Renee and Roxanne just sat at a table drinking and watching in awe as her mother worked through her midlife crisis. The more her mother drank, the sexier her dancing became. The sexier her dancing became, the more the three of them laughed in embarrassment.

All Nicole could think about was that she didn't want to talk about sex with her mother, she didn't want to think about her mother having sex, and she didn't want a repeat of this night ever again. She turned to Roxanne and said, "Promise me you won't let me get to this point."

"Only if you promise me you won't let me get to this point either." They clinked bottles to seal the deal.

"Oh, come on, you guys. She's having fun. She's not hurting anybody. She's with us so she won't get into any trouble."

"Would you feel the same if it were your mother?" Nicole asked.

"Okay, you're right. Promise me you guys won't let me get to this point." They all clinked bottles again.

Nicole's mom came over to the table and guzzled her drink. She grabbed their hands and pulled them out onto the dance floor. The four of them danced until two when they all decided to call it a night. Nicole's mom said she was invited to a party and begged Nicole and the girls to join her. Nicole refused and became the mother. "And you're not going either. We're getting a cab and we're going home."

Nicole and her mother were dropped off first and, a bit unsteadily, they made their way up the stairs to the condo. Nicole made up the hideaway bed while her mother was in the bathroom, then hollered, "Goodnight, Mom. See you in the morning."

"You're not going to wash your face and brush your teeth?"

Nicole rolled her eyes, grabbed a kitchen dish towel and rinsed it out with hot water before she scrubbed her face. She scooped up a handful of hot water and rinsed out her mouth. "There, Mother," she said under her breath and headed to bed closing the bedroom door firmly behind her.

A couple minutes later her mom was tapping at her door. "Honey, I just wanted to say thank you for a great night. I had a lot of fun and can't wait until tomorrow night."

Nicole made a face in the dark, like, yeah right, she'll be hung over and want to go home. "You're welcome, Mom. Thanks for coming to see me. I had fun, too."

The next morning Nicole woke early and decided to take her pregnancy test even though she shouldn't get her period for at least another week. She wasn't late, but she wanted to take the test. She grabbed the bag from her closet shelf and crept quietly to the bathroom. She sat on the toilet with the stick between her legs and peed. She turned and grabbed a few Kleenex to set the stick on, and watched it as she wiped.

She wasn't ready to have a baby. She thought about what Roxanne had said, and Nicole knew she was right. She had to slow down. She didn't want to keep jumping into these flings that didn't last. She didn't want to worry about pregnancy or disease. She thought that maybe she would try dating, get to know somebody, let somebody get to know her.

"Borrr-rrrring," she said out loud and started giggling.

She took another look at the stick and quietly hurried back to the bedroom before her mother woke up. She stashed the used test and wrapper back up in the closet and crawled into bed. She grabbed the phone next to her bed and called Roxanne. The answering machine picked up. "Rox, I've decided you're right. I'll try dating somebody but only if you do the same. Call me back so we can discuss it." Nicole hoped she would be able to get back to sleep.

***

Nicole was sleeping when her mother knocked on her door two hours later.

"Honey, do you have coffee?"

"Uh, no. I always go to Starbucks across the street."

"Okay, I'm going. Do you want anything?"

"Sure, I'd love a vanilla latte."

"Okay, I'll get you one."

Nicole heard her mother leave. She jumped out of bed and grabbed her test out of the closet. She looked at it again. The line still showed that she was not pregnant. Relieved, she opened her window and tossed the test outside into the dumpster. She noticed her condo manager standing in the alley talking to a maintenance worker.

"Hey! When you going to move this dumpster? It stinks!"

Ignoring her, he continued talking to the worker, then they shook hands and the worker walked away. He looked up at her and said, "If you want to talk to me, make an appointment."

"Okay, I'd like to make an appointment. Are you busy now?"

"Call my office."

She slammed the window shut, returned to bed and waited for her mom to come back with coffee. She hoped her mother would want to go home.

Nicole found her phone under the covers and dialed the condo manager's office. Of course, the voicemail picked up because it was Saturday.

"Hi, this is Nicole. I just saw you in the alley. You were too busy to talk to me, but I have a complaint. I want that dumpster moved. If you need me to set up an appointment to tell you that I want that dumpster moved, then fine. Call me so we can set up an appointment so I can tell you that I want that dumpster moved. Thank you. I look forward to your call and especially to our meeting so I can tell you that I want that dumpster moved."

She wanted to slam the phone down, but she could only push the button. So she pushed it very fast and very hard, believing that she conveyed her frustration with him and the dumpster.

Over an hour had passed before her mother returned. Nicole had already showered and tidied up her place. "Mother, what took you so long? I was beginning to worry."

"Oh, Nicole, you're starting to sound like my mother."

"Mother, I wish you would've told me you were going to drink your coffee there. I would've gone with you."

"Oh, no need. I had company."

"What do you mean? Who?"

"I met somebody," she said with a strange smile.

"I don't know what you're getting at, but it doesn't sound good. What are you getting at? You met a guy?" Nicole asked, raising her eyebrows and leaving her mouth open.

"Close your mouth. Yes, I met a guy," she said, with "guy" in quotation marks.

"Mom, you're married! To my dad! What are you thinking?" Nicole started pacing.

"We're having dinner tonight. You girls will have to party without me this evening."

"Oh, no, you're going home!" She turned to the phone to call her dad.

"Don't be a party pooper."

"That's it!" She dialed her parents' phone number and her dad answered. "Dad, Mom is headed home. I have a lot of work to do, and I need to stay focused. Thanks for having her stay with me. We had a great night last night. She has really taken my mind off Tom." Nicole gave her mom a dirty look. "I mean really she has taken my mind off *my* problems."

Her mother rolled her eyes.

"Okay, Dad, I will. I love you, too. Bye." She hung up the phone and turned to her mother. "What is wrong with you? Are you going through a midlife crisis? Are you going to divorce Daddy?"

"Nicole, if you don't want me here, I'll leave."

"Mom, it's not that. It's just that you're acting very strange, and I think you should go home before you get yourself into trouble."

"Is there something wrong with having dinner with a nice Latino gentleman?"

"Ah, yah! You're married!"

"Having dinner is breaking a vow?"

"Does Dad know you want to have dinner with a nice Latino gentleman?"

"Does your father have to know everything about me and what I do when he's not around?"

Nicole took a deep breath and looked up at the ceiling. "I can't do this. You're not making sense to me. You have to go now. Go home. Give Daddy a big hug and tell him you love him."

"I thought you girls were having so much fun… city life. But you are dreary." She started gathering her things together. "Do you want to get a bite to eat before I head back?"

"Sure, Mom. Let me grab my purse."

Chapter 6

WHEN NICOLE GOT back home after lunch with her mom, she headed back to bed to feel sorry for herself. Snuggling in, her mind drifted to her younger years in Cannon Falls.

***

Nicole lived about a mile from the nursing home where her grandpa stayed. She spent as much time with him as she did at home. The waterfalls were a little out of the way, but she always stopped there on her way to visit her grandpa. She'd throw rocks, soak her feet if she was hot or just sit and listen to the water falling. She loved the falls. And her grandpa always asked her, "How are the falls today?"

"They're great, Grandpa!" The happiest times were when her parents would take him for the day and they would picnic by the waterfalls. They threw rocks together and sometimes pretended to fish. There was nothing wrong with her grandpa other than he forgot things sometimes and told funny stories and sometimes called her by her father's name, but that just made her laugh. "Grandpa, that's your son! I'm your granddaughter, silly!"

She was old enough to know that he had been changing, but that sudden change when she was thirteen devastated and angered her. She didn't want to lose her grandpa because he was her best friend.

The time came when he stopped asking her about the falls and all he wanted to talk about was his flowers, his fake plastic flowers that her mother had "planted" just outside his window. Her grandpa stopped being fun. He would sit for hours watching the flowers. He would talk about the new blooms, and the way the flowers swayed in the breeze. She felt crazy every time she left the nursing home because her mother joined in the madness. "Dad, did you see the new pink snapdragons? I saw the bees pollinating them when I came in this morning," her mother would tell him.

Even with snow on the ground, she talked about the perennials and the bulbs that they dug up just in time. Nicole was angry that her grandpa didn't secretly whisper to her, "Come on, Nicole, let's just let them play this little charade; it will be our little game. We all know they're plastic." He never whispered to her; he never stopped the insanity. She used to stare at him and try to bring him back, but he was gone. Her grandpa was gone.

Her parents tried to explain that he had Alzheimer's disease. "Honey, it's not his fault. He still loves you very much."

"But why do you keep pretending those flowers are real! He doesn't care about flowers! Stop it! He doesn't want to talk about the flowers!" Nicole would scream at her parents and sob. She didn't know if she was angrier at her parents for pretending everything was fine or angrier at her grandpa for leaving her.

Then one day on her way to visit him, she only went as far as the waterfalls. She couldn't bring herself to go all the way to the nursing home. She never told her parents that she stopped visiting him. Her grandpa would never know the difference. She spent hours at the falls, lying in the grass, meeting other kids and playing in the water. She savored this new-found rebellion mixed with the music of the river against the rocks and the falling water.

Nicole was growing up, and she refused to visit her grandpa even when her parents did. She was letting go of her friendship with her grandpa and replacing it with friendship with the school and neighborhood kids. She and her friends always ran around trying to get into trouble but never really getting the job done. It was impossible in Cannon Falls, because somebody's parents, neighbors or grandparents always caught them before they did something too terrible. Back then, kids could be spanked by anybody, and Nicole had her share of spankings.

Her grandpa passed away about a year after she stopped visiting him. He choked on a piece of candy. Everybody said it was for the best, but the news devastated Nicole. It felt like she lost him all over again. She felt terrible guilt and regretted not visiting him and talking to him about the flowers. Just to be with him would have been good enough. But now he was really gone.

Her drinking and sexual hookups started not long after her grandpa died. She lost her virginity the day after her fifteenth birthday party with her boyfriend in his parents' house just after they raided the liquor cupboards together.

***

Nicole's phone rang, and she was back to her bedroom in her condo. She wiped away the tears, sat up in bed and let the call go to voicemail.

Nicole started thinking about how sex and drinking went hand in hand from the start. *I love sex and I love drinking, so why not combine the two? It only makes sense.* "Ugh!" she grimaced, rolling over and covering her head with a pillow, trying to block out the thought of what that said about her.

Nicole missed it. She missed all of it. She missed her parents being happy and superhuman in her eyes. She missed her grandpa. She missed the fun and innocent trouble she used to get into with her friends. She even missed the joy of trying to sneak beer from the keg in the neighbor's garage or stealing cans of beer from the back of the case in the refrigerator at one of her friend's houses.

Nicole jumped out of bed and headed straight to the fridge for a beer. She chugged it down, went back to the bedroom and opened the window. "That's so nasty!" she said looking down at the garbage. She let out a huge belch before tossing her empty beer can into the foul dumpster.

She missed the way Minnesota smelled during the summer. She missed the aroma of the freshly cut hay and grass, the scent of the rivers and lakes. She missed the smell of the cotton candy and hotdogs at the Cannon Falls fair. And now all she could smell was the nasty, stinky garbage seeping in through her bedroom window.

Nicole closed the window and got back into bed. She missed the waterfalls and the feeling she used to have while sitting on the grass by the river. It was her favorite place to be. She wondered why she didn't go to the beach more. She wondered if she could find the same comfort from the beach. She doubted it: too many people, too much of a show and if she waited until everybody left, it might be too dangerous. But maybe she'd give it a try someday.

She missed that feeling of safety from small-town living where everybody knows everybody. The whole town went to funerals, graduations and weddings. In Cannon Falls, everybody knew your business, unlike Miami where nobody cares about your business. Nicole kind of liked both—to be cared for and to be left alone.

Nicole thought about the friends she had right before she moved to Naples. The river seemed to be their favorite place to be, too. They used to meet there to drink and lounge on inner tubes. Somebody always found a little alcohol. The move had been tough for Nicole, and she didn't regain her confidence until college where she met Roxanne and Renee and Blaine and Christian. Nicole thought about how lucky she was to have such great friends close by and parents who lived far enough away, yet close enough to be there when she needed them.

She clumsily rolled off her bed and grabbed her phone to check her voicemail. Maybe a night out with friends could bring her out of her funk.

Chapter 7

WHEN NICOLE GOT home from working late on Thursday night, she logged onto Facebook. She was surprised to see a friend request from an old boyfriend she had dated a year after high school. He had disappeared, and the rumor was that he had joined the army. Thinking vaguely that their relationship might be reignited, she accepted his friendship request.

Nicole sent a few private messages to friends, wrote on her wall, then noticed her new friend—her old boyfriend, possibly new boyfriend—had written on her wall, "Did you ever have my kid... after all the times I came in you?"

"Oh, my God!" she moaned as she frantically tried to remove it from her wall. "Oh, my God." When he wanted to chat with her, she blocked it and removed him from her friend list, then went back to her wall to see if it was still there.

That's when she noticed that Christian wanted to chat. She clicked to chat.

"What was that??!!!!" he wrote.

"Oh, God! No!" Nicole typed back to him quickly, "Don't judge me, call me!"

"I'll call you... I'll call you a whore!" he typed back, adding a smiley face.

"Is it still on there? Can you see it?"

"Let me check," he typed.

While Nicole waited, she called Renee to have her check her Facebook wall.

"Nope."

"Oh, thank God," she typed back, and called Roxanne to have her check, too.

"Guurl, you better call me! I haven't seen you since we got back from Paris. How was your VD Party? How's Tom, or I mean Stan?"

"Oh, too much to type. Let's have dinner tonight."

***

That evening, Nicole and Roxanne met Christian and Blaine at the Aventura Mall for dinner. The boys shared their Paris photos and talked about how much they loved Paris, vowing to go back but only if Nicole would go with them. Then they came to the most pressing topic.

"Well, Nicole, you'd better do something after that Facebook mishap," Christian said.

"I was young and dumb, and I guess he didn't know I was on the pill." Trying to avoid the subject and change the subject, Nicole said, "So, Roxanne, is there anybody you're interested in?"

"Wait a minute. What kind of person would write that on your wall?"

"I don't know. What kind of person?" She laughed in embarrassment.

"A psycho!" he said, leaning in close to her.

"Well, the psycho has been blocked."

Roxanne shook her head and stared at Nicole. She closed her eyes before saying, "You're going to date him, aren't you?"

"NO! Ugh! No, I am not. Roxy, we have plans. So who are you interested in?"

"Another teacher. Mark," Roxanne answered.

Nicole grinned. "Oh, my God! You are alive. How long has this been going on?"

"Well, we've made eye contact. We've said our friendly hellos. And we have moved on to small talk. I'm just no good at this. I'm attracted to him, but every time I see him, I get tongue-tied, nervous in the stomach and clumsy."

Christian burst out laughing. "Clumsy?"

"I seem to trip a lot, and drop things around him all the time, and I sometimes run into things."

Roxanne was so serious it was hard not to laugh, but the three of them tried to be sensitive and hide their amusement.

"Honey, like what do you run into?" Christian asked, just dying to hear her answer.

"Well like a… I don't know… a desk… a door…"

It seemed her answer was better than Christian had hoped. Laughing, he had to ask, "Are you a virgin?"

Nicole answered for her. "She's not a virgin, Christian. She's sweet and shy and genuine. I like it. It's refreshing. She is picky about men and it's a good thing. Right, Roxy?"

"Just please help me so I can be a normal adult around him."

"Okay, the weather is an easy one to talk about. And if you can find a way to get him talking, it takes the pressure off you having to talk," Blaine chimed in.

"Yes," Christian added. "Ask him if he had a nice weekend. Ask him if he did anything fun."

Roxanne pulled out a small notebook and started writing their suggestions down.

Blaine and Christian looked at each other in disbelief. Then Christian said, "Well, she is a school teacher."

Nicole gently kicked them under the table, then asked, "Would it be wrong for her to just come right out and say she's a little nervous around him, that she's interested in him, or that she's…"

"Wait a minute," Roxanne interrupted. "I don't even know if I should date somebody I work with."

Blaine gently asked, "Do you think he's interested in you?"

"Yeah, I think so. I mean I'm not one hundred percent sure, but I think so."

"Has he asked you out?"

"He's asked me what I was doing for lunch. He's asked me to join them, a group that goes out after work, for a drink. I think he said something about going to see a movie sometime."

All three agreed that he was interested in Roxanne.

"Okay, this is easy. Next time he asks you out, go. Ask him questions and make him do the talking. It'll get easier." Christian turned to Nicole. "Okay. Your turn, miss thang."

"Oh, yeah well, Rox and I are going out for a drink after we finish dinner." She shook her head and raised her hand saying, "Don't worry about me. I'll meet somebody."

"No, not at a bar. Why don't you meet somebody at the bank, not a customer like Tom but a co-worker?" Blaine asked.

"I'll keep an eye on her," Roxanne said, finishing the last of her lemonade.

"Maybe we better stay with you girls."

"No, because every guy will think we're together. We've done that. You can't go out with me when I'm on a mission to find a boyfriend… or I mean find somebody to date… whatever."

Chapter 8

ONE DRINK TURNED into three for Nicole. Roxanne had a drink with dinner and was now only drinking water; it was her turn to be the designated driver. Nicole was mingling while Roxanne stayed seated at a table. A nice looking man had joined her and sat with her most of the night. Nicole was trying to find somebody to go on a date with. She walked by the bar and pressed herself against one of the guys sitting there. "Don't grab my ass," she said as she slowly passed.

"What?" he said, turning to look at her.

"I said, don't grab my ass as I walk by you."

He and his friend started laughing. "Okay, we won't."

"Okay…" she continued walking past them. "That wasn't any fun… hmmm." She noticed a handsome, dark-haired, stocky man only slightly taller than her coming her way. She made eye contact with him, then reached for the top button on her blouse. She tore it off while he watched. "Could you hold this for me?" she asked, being very sincere.

He chuckled and took her button. "Sure."

Ooo, we gotta live one, she thought as she made her way back to the table to check on Roxanne.

"How's it going, Rox?" Nicole grabbed a chair. "Who was the guy? Is he date-worthy?"

"Yes, he is. We're going to a movie next week."

"Oh, my God! You're kidding me!" She noticed her dark-haired stud heading her way, so she tore off her second button and handed it to him. She turned back to talk to Roxanne.

"So, who is he? What does he do?" She winked at Roxanne. "I'm working on one of my own."

"That button trick gets you into bed, not on a date."

"No, not this time. I have a plan."

"Well, the guy is that teacher. He left because he doesn't drink and doesn't like to be around drunk people. He just came out with a couple of friends for an hour or so."

"Oh, my God! I'm so happy for you." But that was a lie. Nicole suddenly felt alone and defeated. She had gotten used to Roxanne being alone, the one to pity, and she could see it all now, Roxanne was doing everything right; she was just the type of woman that men wanted to marry. Feeling it deep in her gut, she knew that now she was the one Roxanne and Renee would pity. She felt sick. How did Roxanne end up with somebody before her? How could this be happening? "Maybe we should go home."

"I'm ready if you are."

Nicole looked over to search out her stud only to see him talking to a thinner, prettier girl. "Yeah, I'm ready."

When Nicole got home she walked across the street to Starbucks, which was just getting ready to close. As she ordered a vanilla latte, she noticed a cute guy sitting alone reading a book. Waiting for her coffee, she struck up a conversation asking the guy if he was single. He was.

"You know, I haven't been on a date for a long time," Nicole said. "And I was wondering if you would like to meet me here for coffee next Wednesday night."

"I have a tournament on Wednesday night, but how about Thursday?"

"Yeah, that sounds good." Grabbing her coffee, she introduced herself. "My name's Nicole."

"I'm Ernie."

She didn't expect that name, but suddenly it was all making sense. He wore glasses and was reading a book that had something to do with green.

She didn't know if he was a vegetarian or learning about living green but somehow she knew, and she was afraid to ask. "What kind of tournament?"

"Oh, Xbox."

"Of course," she said with a nervous giggle. "Good luck. And I'll see you Thursday. Oh, what time?"

"How's seven?"

"Seven-thirty?"

"Sure. I'll see you then, Nicole."

She waved and walked out the door and across the street to her condo building. Walking into the lobby to check her mail, she thought she heard her own voice, so she followed it. It led her to the manager's office. His door was slightly open, and she could see him sitting at his desk by himself listening to the message she had left. "...so we can set up an appointment so I can tell you that I want that dumpster moved. Thank you. I look forward to your call and especially to our meeting so I can tell you that I want that dumpster moved." Her message stopped playing, and she heard him laughing. He pushed a button, and her message played again.

"Hi, this is Nicole. I saw you today in the alley. You were too busy to talk to me, but I have a complaint. I want that dumpster moved. If you need me to set up an appointment to tell you that I want that dumpster moved, then fine. Call me so we can set up an appointment so I can tell you that I want that dumpster moved. Thank you. I look forward to your call and especially to our meeting so I can tell you that I want that dumpster moved." He laughed during her entire message this time.

"Great, he listens to my message almost a week later," Nicole muttered. But not having the energy to confront him, she turned back to the lobby and walked up the stairs to her condo. She had a message on her answering machine. "Nicole this is Joy. If you build it, they will come! I met the most amazing man tonight! He has huge hands—and feet! Call me!"

Nicole turned on her laptop and the TV. She checked her email, then started to Google different topics that had been on her mind, beginning with Xbox. When her mom was in town Friday night, she had mentioned wanting to go to the theater, so Nicole looked up the price of tickets and dates available. Her mother's birthday was right around the corner. She would prefer going to the theater with her mother instead of the bar. Next she looked up diets and exercise. She wondered if she had the discipline anymore to actually follow a diet or exercise regimen. She usually just cut back when she noticed her clothes getting tighter or a few extra pounds on the scale. She promised herself that she would seriously consider walking again, joining a gym or going to the little gym they had in the condo complex.

Nicole remembered the DVD player she had stuck in the drawer of her nightstand. The player was still a little dirty from the dumpster, and she could now see that it was clearly used, meaning that Tom probably got a new one or just didn't want it anymore so he used it to break up with her. She hit play and noticed a crack going across the upper left side of the screen, but it still worked.

"I'm just going to say it: I used you. You were easy, very easy. You did what I wanted when I wanted. You gave me sex whenever I wanted it. I didn't want a relationship, and I thought you knew that. But then you mentioned this party. You're cute, but you're not my type. Don't call me crying…"

Nicole only watched and listened to the first minute of the DVD before she opened her bedroom window and threw it out as hard as she could into the dumpster, trying to break it. She closed the window and felt something warm between her legs. "Oh, please, let it be." She raced into the bathroom and pulled down her pants. There it was, a red smear in her panties.

Nicole finished her coffee, turned on her stereo and she started dancing around her condo. Suddenly, Roxanne and her teacher didn't matter, her laughing condo manager didn't matter, Tom and his DVD didn't matter and Joy's big-handed man didn't matter.

Nicole had dodged one bullet, but she still had one to go.

Chapter 9

THE NEXT WEEK at work was uneventful. She was only yelled at once by her boss, which, Nicole was pretty certain, made it a record week; she usually criticized her at least once a day. But in Nicole's personal life, it was a week to remember.

Roxanne was in love and already going steady with Mark. Roxanne was spending more time talking to Renee and less time talking to her. Nicole understood because both were in relationships and she was not—odd man out.

She had her first date with Ernie and planned another Starbucks meeting the following Thursday, same time, same place, but Nicole figured she would cancel. She thought Ernie was super sexy in a different sort of way, but there was no spark and they had nothing in common. He liked Xbox and hybrid cars and vegans, and Nicole didn't know what she liked. She thought she liked drinking, sex and junk food, but maybe in reality she didn't have an identity. Ernie was a really nice guy, but they were better off as friends.

The best part of her week was when she got that phone call from Planned Parenthood. Her very own cervix-loving doctor called her to give her the news—all of her test results came back negative. She told Nicole that she was proud of her for being concerned, getting checked and especially for practicing safe sex. But she did suggest that Nicole come back to Planned Parenthood in six months for another HIV test, just to be sure. Relieved, Nicole promised she would come back for another test, and hung up feeling grateful for Planned Parenthood. Even after Nicole started making more money and had better insurance, she never even considered going anyplace else. She loved Planned Parenthood because she had always been treated with dignity and respect no matter what she was going through. Planned Parenthood made her feel proud of her body, her choices and her gender.

Friday evening, before a blind date with a friend of Roxanne's new man, Nicole finally had an appointment with her condo manager, Rick the Dick. He told her the dumpster would be there indefinitely. The board was working on a remodeling plan and they were having a hard time agreeing, so everything had been stalled. His hands were tied. He said he was sorry, but she knew he didn't mean it.

"I guess if you don't like it, you can move."

"That's my home! I own that condo!" Nicole did love her building, her condo and especially her location.

"Well, then, I guess you'll be staying. That's nice. Is there anything else I can help you with?" he said, checking his watch.

Nicole was at a loss for words. "No, that's it." She stood up. "Oh, can I join the board?"

"You can sit in. Our meeting is every first Thursday of the month at six-thirty here in the boardroom."

She tried to calculate in her head. "This coming Thursday?"

"The first Thursday of every month," he said, barely acknowledging her.

She slammed her hand against the door making a huge thud, louder than she had expected. She could see that Rick the Dick jumped. "Is that this Thursday?"

"Yes. Will you please close my door?"

She slammed his door, and heard him laughing behind it. Nicole was pissed. She reached for her cell phone and called Renee. "You're wrong! You said whenever somebody is nice to me, if a guy shows interest in me, then I start liking him. Well I have news for you: They can be mean to me, too. It doesn't matter—be nice, be mean, I'll still like 'em all!"

"What happened? And who is it? Be quick, I'm in the middle of a color."

"I'm just fucked, Renee. Some guy is being a total jerk to me and I've never felt more attracted to the man. What's wrong with me?"

Renee giggled. "Nothing, honey, you're wonderful! Sometimes we want what we can't have. You're a go-getter, working girl like me. It used to be the men who wanted a challenge. It sounds like this could be a good thing. You want a challenge in your life. Maybe it has nothing to do with the jerk. Maybe you just want to be challenged."

"Thanks, Renee. You're right."

"That's okay, baby; call me anytime. But for now I have to go and get this woman out from under the dryer."

Nicole hung up the phone and turned around. Rick the Dick had been there the whole time, listening to her conversation. She was totally humiliated.

He smiled at her and nodded his head.

Nicole's mind raced, *What did I say? What did I just say? Oh, God… what did he hear me say?* She couldn't remember anything except something about a challenge in her life. "I'm going to start an exercise plan… a challenge." As soon as she heard the word, challenge, she knew it wasn't she who had said that word out loud, but Renee. Her mind raced until she remembered that she had said something about a mean guy that she thought was hot, or something like that. "Oh," she laughed, "this guy I know is mean to me." She laughed some more. "And I like it." When she realized what she had just said, Nicole dashed up the stairs, rushed into her condo and flopped onto the couch, all the while laughing hysterically. "I have got to be the biggest dork in the world."

She was still laughing when the phone rang. It was her father. "Honey, I'm trying to get tickets for you and your mother to go to the theater for her birthday. So could you do me a huge favor and leave a few dates open in case I manage this?"

"Dad, that's so funny because I was going to do the same thing. But I know the show she wanted to see is sold out, and I couldn't get tickets."

"Oh, well, if I get them, they can be from both of us. And I know she'd rather go with you than me, so leave the third weekend of the month open, okay?"

"You got it, Dad."

"She's had such a great time with you."

"I'm glad. I have, too," she lied.

"Okay, honey, I better get going. I love you and I miss you. When are you coming to visit me?"

"Soon, Dad."

"All right, honey. Well, have a great weekend."

"You, too, Daddy. Love you."

Nicole hung up the phone feeling a little uneasy. She couldn't put her finger on it, but she didn't like the way he'd said, "She's had a great time…" It sounded like she'd made more than one trip to Miami to visit her. But she brushed it off, thinking that she was just being paranoid.

Nicole hoped that one day she would have a man as great as her daddy. Maybe she would meet him tonight on her blind date. She turned on her stereo and jumped in the shower to get ready for her night of possibilities.

Chapter 10

MARK HAD ASKED Roxanne and Nicole to meet him and his friend, Frank, aka a blind date, at the AA arena for a Miami Heat basketball game. Because of her appointment with Rick the Dick, Nicole had to meet the others there. When she arrived, she was pleasantly surprised. Frank looked good, dressed nicely and smelled great; he was just her type.

Roxanne and Nicole sat between the two guys and there wasn't much talking. It was Nicole's first time meeting Mark, who seemed like a nice guy. Roxanne and Mark were clearly crazy about each other, and a good match. Nicole was happy for her, but a little jealous. It was strange to see her with somebody because she had been alone for a long time.

Nicole noticed one of the rich, fancy girls sitting close by wearing a little skirt and high heels. Noticing her shoes first, she looked up her leg and saw cellulite dimpling her thigh. She hesitated, but had to do it. She pointed her out to Frank, saying, "Oh, I'd be so cold if I were her." Just as she said it, the beautiful young woman uncrossed her legs and there was no trace of cellulite. So Frank took a good, hard look and missed the most important part of what she wanted him to see—that even young beautiful women in short skirts have cellulite.

Nicole kept eyeing the guy walking around with pink and blue cotton candy. She would settle for either, but didn't know how to get his attention, mostly because she didn't want to look like a pig in front of Frank or Mark. Her mouth watered as she watched him walk around selling the pastel dream on a stick. Did adults even eat cotton candy or was it a treat for kids only? How foolish would she look if she yelled him over and bought a bag? Then she had a great idea: She would get some before the game was over, say it was for her nephew and then eat it on the drive home. But did she really want to start a relationship by lying to him before she even knew him? What if he were the one? What if she later had to confess that she didn't have a nephew, and she didn't have any sisters or brothers? But she didn't care. Nicole raised her hand just as her blind date raised his. Frank didn't notice, as he waved over the cotton candy guy.

Nicole thought she had gone to heaven. Frank was perfect in every way. But then he didn't ask her if she wanted any. He didn't even look at her as he paid the guy and said, "I love this stuff."

What a jerk. He'd better share.

Frank sat next to her stuffing his face with *her* blue, fluffy sugar. And if that wasn't bad enough, his elbow kept bumping her breast each time he took a mouthful, reminding her of what she was missing. Then he leaned over and offered some to Mark, who passed. Frank offered it to Roxanne and she passed, too. Nicole was about to have an oral orgasm when he finally offered her some. She could not believe what came out of her mouth. "Oh, no thank you. That's a little too sweet for me."

What the fuck just happened! Nicole got up and excused herself, saying she had to go to the bathroom. She went straight into the walkway looking for food and found a place that sold the unattainable cotton candy. She ordered a bag of pink and went straight into the bathroom to eat it. She stood by the sinks and didn't care who saw her. She was thankful that Roxanne didn't decide to join her. The sugary, sweet cotton melted in her mouth. It was the best cotton candy she had ever had.

Nicole thought about Frank and really didn't think she could date somebody so selfish. He had waited until his cotton candy was almost gone before he started offering it to the others. Of course nobody was going to have any when there wasn't much left. And the way he was licking his fingers. "That's disgusting," she said as she licked her own fingers.

Nicole noticed how pretty and skinny all the girls were that were coming in and out of the ladies room. Their bodies were perfect; their jewelry and clothes were perfect; their hair was perfect; and they appeared to have perfect lives. Who wouldn't when they looked like that? She looked down at herself and compared her figure and her clothes to the beautiful women who had just left.

She wasn't the only one looking. They were checking her out, too, only with a little pity in their eyes. She figured they were thinking, *Cute face, if only she'd lose some weight,* or *Poor lonely, fat girl, stuffing her face with cotton candy.* Nicole wasn't a threat, but some of the other women were, and it was obvious by the hostile looks they gave each other. Nicole figured they compared the labels on their jeans, percentages of their body-fat, and sizes of their diamond rings and implants. She loved women like that because she totally understood. And deep down as much as Nicole wanted to be one of those fancy, snobby women, she knew she was a Midwestern, corn-fed woman who would never quite fit in to that lifestyle. She also knew that she would probably always care more about sneaking a bag full of cotton candy than fitting into a pair of two-hundred-dollar jeans.

Nicole didn't get to see this side of Miami often because she worked and lived too far west. But she always enjoyed it when she did find her way to the beaches, malls and restaurants of South Beach.

When the game was over, Frank asked Nicole and the others to join him for a bite to eat at a nearby restaurant. Roxanne and Mark didn't want to, but Nicole did. She figured it would give her a chance to get to know him. They ordered nachos to share and a beer each. Sitting across from him, Nicole reminded herself that getting to know somebody was what dating was all about, so she started asking him questions about himself: Where do you live? What do you like to do with your free time? What do you do for a living? Do you have any brothers or sisters?

After his third beer, Frank started getting a little louder and more aggressive. Nicole kind of liked it, because she thought it showed that he was passionate. But about twenty minutes into a discussion they were having about a fight he'd had with a co-worker, Nicole found herself looking around smiling and nodding at other patrons, trying to reassure them that she was fine.

"You son-of-a-bitch!" Frank said loudly, pointing his finger in Nicole's face.

Nicole ducked her head in embarrassment, glancing to see if anybody was staring.

"I told you to get off my ass!" Frank continued. "I'll tell YOU when this deal goes through!"

Nicole laughed nervously.

"You better back off or I'll kick your fuck'n ass!" he shouted, shaking his fist toward Nicole.

Nicole quickly grabbed his hand as if really digging him. "Oh, my God. You were really upset, weren't you?" Nicole pretended that she wanted to hold his hands. "Are you going to get fired?"

"Fuck no! I run the place, and he knows that!" He smiled at her. "Should we get going?" he asked. He seemed thrilled that she was still holding his hand, but she was too afraid to let go. She thought somebody was going to call the cops about a domestic situation.

"I had a great time," she said as they walked to their cars. Though she didn't see him as relationship material, she really wanted to have sex with him. His testosterone was out of control, and it was scary and sexy at the same time.

They talked for a few minutes outside of the restaurant before he moved in to kiss her. His lips were tight and hard, and her desire to take him home with her vanished. How could this be? She kissed him again, but his lips didn't seem to be there. She backed away to take a look, but his lips looked normal; he had nice, normal lips. "Hmm?" She smiled because she hadn't meant to make a noise.

He smiled back. "It was nice meeting you. Let's do it again sometime."

"Sure." She nodded and waved goodbye as she walked to her car. She knew that, "Let's do it again sometime," really meant, "What a waste of a night," especially when he didn't ask for her number or ask if he could call her.

Nicole drove away wishing she could get her hands on another bag of cotton candy. Even though she didn't care much for him, she couldn't stop wondering why he didn't like her. Was it because she wasn't skinny? Did she say something wrong? Was there something wrong with *her* kiss? She tried to convince herself that it was just the wrong chemistry, nothing wrong with her, nothing wrong with him, just a bad fit. She didn't know if she liked the dating thing. It was easier to just hop into bed and then figure it out later; at least then she got some fun out of the deal. She tried to laugh, but could only smile meekly. She pulled down her visor mirror to look at herself while waiting at a stop light. Same, she looked the same.

Nicole's eyes filled with tears. She felt rejected and empowered at the same time. All sorts of emotions raced through her. She wondered if sex was love to her in some way. She wondered if she was a narcissist and if she really didn't want to take the time to get to know somebody else. Maybe she was a user; maybe she wanted a good time from men and nothing more. Did she even like men?

This dating thing wasn't going to be easy, but she could still see why it was a good idea.

Chapter 11

NICOLE WOKE EARLY on Saturday morning and decided to go for a quick thirty-minute walk. When she got back to her building, she went to the gym, which was really just a room with a stationary bike and a universal cable and weight exercise machine. She read through the different exercises she could do on just the one machine; she could work virtually every muscle. She was a little surprised by how much fun she was having doing something good for herself. Nicole was just about finished with her workout when Rick the Dick stuck his nosey head into the gym to see who was in there.

"You were serious, about the challenge thing."

Nicole took a good long, hard look at him to see if there was anything about him that was attractive. His brown hair was thinning on top, but it looked okay because he kept it short and wasn't trying to hide the fact that he is losing his hair. His eyes were a light color, green or grayish. His skin was nice, and he looked good with a haven't-shaved-for-a-day look.

She suddenly realized that he wasn't there to check on the gym; he was there to use it. He was wearing long shorts and a t-shirt with flip-flops. His body was gorgeous. She could see it now that he wasn't in his typical slacks, white shirt and a tie. Or maybe she was finally looking. "Do you live here? Because this gym is for the owners."

"Well, it's good to have a watchdog like you around, Nicole, but, yes, I live here. Condo 234."

Nicole was immediately pissed about the watchdog comment. *Obviously he thinks I'm a dog. Nice.* She suddenly understood what it felt like to be tongue-tied, something she had never experienced before in her life. She didn't have a comeback. She wasn't witty and she most definitely wasn't friendly. She struggled to speak, then blurted, "You know, I'm sorry. I think we got off on the wrong foot. I have nothing against you, but I do have something against having a dumpster below my bedroom window. It really stinks sometimes, I mean horribly. I've bought so many of those air freshener plug-ins and spray. Oh, my God, you can't imagine how much air freshener I've bought to mask the odor from seeping up into my room. It's not always bad. But I still really wish that dumpster could be moved."

Suddenly, Nicole couldn't stop talking. "I have sprayed a whole can of that spray out the window, outside into the air. Isn't that crazy? See that dumpster is causing me to go insane. It's not all bad; sometimes it's handy. I just open my window and throw things out. Like the other day," Nicole's mind was screaming *Shut up! Shut up!* but she couldn't get her mouth to close. "I was eating cookie dough and heard on the news that raw cookie dough, I don't know, something about E-coli poisoning. So I grabbed another spoonful before I threw it... and the spoon... out the window right into the dumpster... No, not really. Well, I mean I did throw it out the window, but I didn't take another bite first. I thought about it," she laughed, "but I didn't." She laughed some more. "I'm just trying to say..."

Thank God he interrupted her. "Cookie dough really isn't that good for you."

"I know, but comfort food..."

"I'm not sure it really qualifies as food."

Nicole was getting frustrated because she couldn't say what she wanted to say. Everything came out wrong. "I better go. Have a nice workout." She took a few steps toward the door.

"How's that mean man treating you?" he asked. "Horrible, I hope." He grinned at her.

She smiled back and left the room.

When Nicole got back to her condo she had the urge to purge and clean just like her body had finished doing a few days earlier. This was one of the first Saturdays Nicole had no plans, and she was happy about it. She wanted to spend the day cleaning, organizing closets and throwing out her fat clothes. She had kept some of her favorite fat outfits from when she was still in college when she was at her biggest. She was afraid to let them go just in case. But she knew it was time.

Nicole decided to start in her bedroom, possibly the root cause of some of her issues. She stripped her bed, then decided to flip the mattress. She had never done it before and heard people say that you should. But the main reason she wanted to flip the mattress was to have the fresh side up, the side that no men had been on. Turning her mattress would symbolize a fresh, man-less, memory-less place to sleep.

She lifted the mattress and leaned it against the wall. There was something black lying at the edge of her box spring. As she held up the t-shirt, she read AC/DC. It had to have been Stan's, which he must have tucked under her mattress at some point. "What a freak," she said out loud, then immediately started thinking, *Then what does that make me; I shared my bed with him.* She went straight to the window, opened it and tossed the t-shirt into the dumpster.

Next Nicole started working on her bedroom closet. She pulled out her fat clothes that were so neatly hidden, hanging in the back against the wall. She started with her pants. The clothes that she'd thought she would regret getting rid of didn't look so cute after all. She tried on a few pairs of pants and a couple of dresses. Emotionally, she had outgrown them; physically, they had outgrown her. And she was ready to let them go. One by one, she tossed them out her window into the dumpster. She figured by not taking them to Goodwill she was doing somebody a favor, and she felt the need for the symbolism of dumping these things out of her life and into the dumpster.

Nicole cleaned out her dresser drawers, throwing out old bras, panties, socks and pajamas that would be too embarrassing to wear. Anything stretched, torn or stained went straight out the window. She threw out all her old sex toys and games she came across, but she did keep her one good vibrator and a little KY jelly. Nicole also kept all the condoms she had: the condoms from Planned Parenthood, some she'd bought a while back and the large condoms she bought that day she met Joy. Her nightstand drawer was full of old notes and cards from family, friends and old boyfriends.

After reading a few, she removed the drawer and dumped its entire contents out the window into the dumpster. She put the drawer back and filled it with the condoms, vibrator and KY.

Nicole turned on her stereo, then headed to her kitchen, figuring everything would be fine in her cupboards and drawers because she hardly cooked or ate at home. She was right. The only things to toss were an old box of cereal she didn't like and an old jar of vitamins that she couldn't take because they were too big to swallow. She cleaned and rearranged her refrigerator, surprised at how many things had expired: mayonnaise, spaghetti sauce, ketchup and some raspberry jelly. She didn't think she'd used any of them for a year at least. She didn't even know why she had them, so out the window they all went.

The bathroom, on the other hand, needed some work. It always surprised her how she could be so clean and organized at work—one of the things she prided herself on and made her one of the top personal bankers at her branch—but how messy and cluttered she could be in her bathroom. The shelves were crammed with products she didn't use but didn't want to throw out in case she would need them. She went back into the kitchen for a garbage bag.

She cleaned out the shower, under the sink, the three drawers, the medicine cabinet and the linen closet. By the time she was finished, she had two garbage bags full of half-used makeup, lotions and creams, old pink razors, scrubby sponges and luffas and half-empty bottles of numerous types of soaps, shampoos and conditioners. Nicole carried the two bags straight to her bedroom window and tossed them into the dumpster.

Nicole looked around her condo. Her purging had left her feeling clean and in control. She loved her place. Nicole had bought her condo only about a year and a half ago, when she felt her job was stable and was certain of the location she wanted to live in. Both Roxanne and Renee lived close by. Her building was close to her work as well as to countless restaurants and bars. She bought her condo while the old building was being overhauled, with the apartments being remodeled and sold as condos. When she looked at hers, it was gutted and being sold as is. She got a great deal and, with help from everybody she knew, she turned the old dumpy, empty space into the most beautiful condo in the building—she was sure of it. All the rooms were large, but there was only one bedroom and one bathroom. Nicole figured for the price, location and space, it was a great first home.

Her parents helped her with her down payment as an early house-warming gift. Christian and Blaine had convinced her to buy it and assured her that they could make it beautiful. They saw possibilities where Nicole saw only cement floors and drywall. Roxanne searched out where to buy good quality granite, hardwood and everything else at their cheapest. And Renee had a client who was a contractor who oversaw the entire project. It was a small job for him, so his wife did most of the work with Christian's help. In exchange, Renee had to give them both free cuts and color for a year. Renee and Nicole tallied it up, and Nicole happily wrote her a check. It saved her thousands of dollars and thousands of headaches.

Thanks to Christian and Blaine, she had all stainless-steel appliances, cherry cabinets and granite countertops. They rearranged the kitchen and knocked down a wall to give her an open floor plan and a breakfast-bar area. Her bathroom also had the same cabinets and granite vanity top. She had a large soaking tub and a walk-in shower with glass doors. She loved the brushed satin finish of the lighting fixtures, hardware and faucets throughout her condo. She had chosen dark hardwood for the living areas and beige carpet for the bedroom. When it was clean and organized, which it usually was, she thought her place was beautiful enough to be used as a show home or to be featured in a magazine—except for the foul smell in her bedroom every time she opened her window. Nicole grabbed some air freshener from her bedroom closet and sprayed the entire can out her window toward the dumpster.

After a quick shower, she put on shorts and a t-shirt and headed to Starbucks with a book she'd found while she was cleaning. She ordered her usual, then sank into a comfortable chair and started reading her long-lost book, a contemporary romance novel that seemed to be more about shopping and shoes and living in Manhattan than romance. But it did the job of distracting her from her current man troubles.

About twenty minutes later, she heard somebody ask, "Is this seat taken?"

She glanced up, saying, "No, help yourself," and realized that it was Rick. "Oh, hi," she said, noticing that the place was empty and he could have sat anywhere.

He reached into the folder he was carrying. "I saw you sitting here, so I thought I would give you a copy of the agenda for Thursday's meeting." He handed her the sheet, then sat down.

"Oh, thanks." She glanced at it. "I've never seen you at Starbucks before."

"I'm an odd one. I skip the morning coffee and occasionally enjoy an afternoon fix."

"Oh, and I rarely have an afternoon coffee, but today I'm celebrating."

"What are you celebrating?"

"I'm celebrating that I have absolutely no plans the rest of my weekend, and I'm loving it. I've already cleaned my entire condo from top to bottom. I found this book in my closet, so I'm going to read it."

"That does sound nice. I don't think I've ever had a weekend like that."

"It's rare. One of my best friends is swamped with work; she's a stylist and has some big event coming up. The other is in a new relationship, so she's always busy," she said and smiled. "So here I am. I may catch a movie later. I haven't been to a movie for a long time."

"Well, I'll let you get back to your book… and your quiet day."

"Okay, thanks for the sheet. I'm looking forward to Thursday." She took a sip of her coffee. "You think I can stir 'em all up and get that dumpster out of there?"

He smiled and shook his head. "You can try. But I think you like the dumpster. I've seen a lot of activity coming from your bedroom window."

The smile faded from Nicole's face and panic set in as Rick walked out of Starbucks. Waiting until he crossed the street and went into the building, she dashed across the street and ran up the one flight of stairs to her condo. She almost never took the elevator because it was too slow. She passed her door on the right and kept walking, searching for Condo 234 and praying that it would be on the left side of the hall. She turned the corner to the right and noticed a couple of doors missing numbers. She kept walking and there it was to the right. She sat down on the floor facing his door and banged her head against the wall. From the alley his condo was diagonal from hers, so he could see everything coming out of her window.

Her mind raced. *Okay, so he saw me throw out ketchup and mayonnaise and two bags of bathroom trash. So what?* "Oh, God," she moaned when she remembered the vibrator and feather duster and sex toys and sex games, her old bras and stained underwear, and her fat clothes.

She went back further. *What if he saw me stuck in the dumpster in my red teddy and tennis shoes? And Stan pushing on my ass?* "Oh, God, no wonder he laughs at me all the time." She closed her eyes and threw her head back against the wall again.

"Are you lost?" Rick asked, standing there smiling at her, holding his coffee in one hand and his keys in the other.

"No… you live right here," she said flatly.

"Yes, Condo 234."

"The dumpster is not far from your window either."

"Well, it's a little further, but I do know the smell you keep talking about." He offered her a hand to help her up. "Unfortunately, I don't have near the fun that you have with that dumpster."

Nicole stood up and let go of his hand as a wave of humiliation flooded over her, she realized he wasn't her friend; he just loved laughing at her. He was the biggest dick she had ever known. She hurried past him, down the hall and into her condo. "Okay, that's it! I'm going to avoid him like the plague!" She ran straight into her bedroom and closed the blinds.

Chapter 12

BY THAT THURSDAY, Nicole wished she had kept her date with Ernie. At least then she would have a legitimate reason to miss the meeting. Nicole had two options: she could continue ignoring Rick the Dick, ignore the meeting and go on about her life, or she could pull herself together and walk into the meeting in a professional manner as she would for work and forget about Rick the Dick and how he had humiliated her or, more accurately, how she had humiliated herself.

At ten-thirty she knew she would not go to the meeting. Then on her lunch break she was certain that she would. At two o'clock, she was sure that she would not go to the board meeting. And by six that evening she was getting ready for the meeting. She freshened her makeup, perfume and deodorant. She fixed her hair and added some hairspray. She re-tucked her blouse into her skirt and took a quick look in the mirror. She repeated to herself, "This is about the dumpster. It is not about the big Dick. This is about the dumpster. It is not about the big Dick." She picked up her Day-Timer, a notebook and her favorite pen and headed to the condo board meeting.

Nicole, an outsider, was coolly welcomed by the six others who attended. The president, vice-president, secretary and treasurer sat at one end of the table and Rick was at their end. Only one other person was there, a concerned owner who had some issues. She was older, Nicole's mom's age, and she was very nice. Nicole was thankful that she wasn't the only one at her end of the table. But it didn't take her long to realize that she, too, was a regular. They all knew each other, reinforcing Nicole's feelings of being an outsider sitting in on *their* meeting. She kept quiet and listened as the president went over the agenda. When he had finished and Nicole raised her hand to ask about the dumpster, she was cut off.

"I will take questions at the end of the meeting. We have a lot to cover tonight."

The woman sitting next to her gave her a sympathetic look and winked at her. It made Nicole feel a little more at ease. Pulling out her agenda, notebook and her pen with purple ink, she started taking notes. She avoided making eye contact with Rick, pretending he wasn't there.

About twenty minutes later, Nicole's cell phone rang. The meeting stopped and all eyes turned to her. Seeing it was Roxanne, she said, "I'm sorry, this is a very important call; I need to get it," and left the room. Out in the hall, she walked away from the boardroom so she wouldn't bother their precious meeting. "Hey, Roxy! Are we still on for tomorrow night?"

"Yes, and I can't wait! I've missed you guys and I have so much to tell you."

"I've missed you and Renee, too, and I have nothing to tell you."

"Are you busy? You sound a little off."

"No, I'm not busy. I'm sitting in on my first condo board meeting, and I'm glad you called because it was boring me to death," she said laughing.

"Glad I could help. Is it about the dumpster?"

"Yes, but I don't think they are going to let me talk. The president claims I can ask a question at the end of the meeting, but I have a feeling that they will run out of time and brush me off."

"Sounds about right. I used to sit in on mine."

"You did?" Nicole was surprised. "Why?"

"I don't know. It gave me something to do."

"Oh, my God! Is that why I'm sitting in?"

"No, you have a legitimate complaint. Besides, you always have stuff to do."

"I don't know, I don't think I had anything better to do." She laughed. "What's happening to me?"

"Oh, I can't wait to hear about how the dating is going."

"You may be disappointed because there isn't much to tell."

"Well, I'm going to call Renee. We're meeting at my place for dinner at seven, right?"

"Yep, I'll be there."

Nicole walked back into the meeting, grabbed her things and left the room. She heard Rick say, "Excuse me." And he came out after her. "Is everything all right?"

"Yes, fine." She kept walking and didn't look back.

She dropped off her Day-Timer and notebook, changed into a pair of jeans and some strappy sandals and left for some Chinese food and maybe a movie afterward.

While at the restaurant, Nicole noticed that everybody was in a couple or a group. She felt independent, and she liked it. Because she had been exercising all week by going for brisk morning walks, she decided to chose something healthy for her meal. Instead of ordering everything fried, she ordered her chicken grilled and her veggies and rice steamed.

She opened her novel. Nicole became so absorbed in the story that she missed the start time of the movie she wanted to see. So instead she ordered an espresso and continued reading. About twenty minutes later, Nicole jumped up and hurried to the bathroom, fearful that she wouldn't make it. She quickly made her toilet paper protective nest and sat down just in time to expel a loud, long fart. "Oh," she said in embarrassment in case she wasn't the only one in the bathroom. She decided to stay put and continue reading her book because her stomach still felt a little off.

Nicole relaxed and felt like she was about to go when somebody came into the bathroom. Her butt puckered. *Great.* There was no way she would be able to go when someone else was in the bathroom. She impatiently waited for the pisser to finish washing her hands. But, of course, she had to fix her makeup and brush her hair. Nicole wished there was some type of public bathroom etiquette: If somebody is in the bathroom trying to take a dump, you must pee, wash your hands and get out of the room as quickly as possible.

The primper left.

Okay, where was I. After trying to relax now that she was alone again, Nicole started to push slightly and was able to go. She flushed immediately even though she didn't think she was finished. Another rule for the Ladies

Public Bathroom Handbook: Keep flushing even before you've finished to eliminate excess odor.

Nicole heard the door open again. *Great!* This time it was another shitter in the stall next to hers. Nicole could tell the way she pushed her pants all the way down to the floor that she had plans to be there for a while. Nicole didn't stand a chance to finish, so she wiped again, flushed again, washed her hands and got out of there as quickly as possible. She felt a little better but decided to head straight home so she would be close to her own toilet, praying she didn't have food poisoning or the flu.

When Nicole got home, she had a message. "Hi, Nicole. Your friend Renee gave me your number and said you might be up for a blind date. Well, it wouldn't be a blind date really for me because I saw your picture while I was sitting in her chair. If you're interested, give me a call." Nicole started laughing. He didn't leave his name or his phone number. She liked him already.

Chapter 13

AT SEVEN O'CLOCK, Nicole and Renee were standing at Roxanne's door, each holding a bottle of wine. They all were dressed up for the occasion. Roxanne looked more beautiful than Nicole had ever seen her—she was glowing in a red, tight-fitting cocktail dress. Renee was in her typical little black dress and Nicole wore the same black dress she had worn for her Valentine's party a few months earlier.

Renee and Nicole looked at each other. Knowing that something was on Roxanne's mind, they asked, "What's going on, Roxy?"

"Spill it," Renee added.

She turned her back to them, adjusted something with her hands, and quickly turned back and held out her hand. "We're engaged."

"In what?" Nicole said before she understood. She stared at Roxanne who was starting to cry. "Oh, my God!" Nicole said and started to cry, too.

After hugging each other, they admired Roxanne's ring. "It's beautiful!" Renee breathed.

"How did he propose?" Nicole asked, wiping her eyes.

"Let's sit down and eat, and I'll tell you all about it."

They learned that before the engagement, Mark had taken her to the mall where they'd casually ended up looking at rings in jewelry stores. Roxanne now realized that he was trying to get a feel for the type of ring she would want. The night Mark proposed, he took her out to dinner and after dinner they went back to her place. Roxanne was certain that it would be the night they would make love for the first time. She was right, but only after he got down on one knee and asked her to marry him, and she had said yes. Then they made mad, passionate love the rest of the night. "It was perfect," she said, gazing lovingly at her ring. "I did want a traditional ring, solitaire and a band, so it was easy for him to pick the right one. I love it. We're thinking next May."

Nicole and Renee were speechless. Neither said what they were thinking, *Do you think it's too soon?*

"Okay then, now that you're getting married, I need to give you some advice," Renee said. "I know you're not going to want to hear this." Renee took a sip of wine. "Don't play nicey, nicey right off the bat because you'll get sick of it quickly. For example, you need two TVs in the bedroom, both with headsets. That way, you can be together but watch what you want to watch."

Nicole laughed. "I never thought about that. I don't even have a TV in my bedroom."

"Let me finish," Renee said. "Forget everything you ever learned about being selfless in a relationship, that you should always give in, give, give, give, that's how you make a relationship work. Absolutely not! Somebody's going to do the giving and somebody's going to do the taking. Women tend to be the givers and men the takers. It's like they think women were created to follow a man, or be his little friend who does whatever he says." She rolled her eyes. "I'm serious now. I had to go through this with Jason, so listen to me. Learn from my mistakes. I gave, then waited for him to give, but he never did. So I resented him and threw a big fit, but that didn't do any good either. So I decided two can play this game. I started doing what-ever, whenever I wanted. I stopped doing everything he wanted, and now, guess what? We both give and take." She leaned closer to Roxanne. "Roxy, you need to hear this more than Nicky, because you're too nice sometimes. So let him know right away that you have your own likes and dislikes and just because you're married doesn't mean you suddenly love everything he loves."

"It's not like that at all! He's very giving."

"They are at first. I'm telling you, this is important. I don't know what it is about these guys, but women need to be more like them. We need to be selfish in our relationships because it's the only way we'll be happy."

"He really is giving. I'm not just saying it." She squeezed Renee's arm. "He really is."

Renee shrugged and said, "Okay, that's fine, but file it. You'll need it down the road. And I won't say I told you so."

"Okay, I'll file it."

"Thank you." She looked at Nicole. "You're quiet."

"Listening and learning," she said smiling.

"Okay, so that brings us to number two: Never fake an orgasm, I mean never! You do it once, and he'll think he's better in bed than he is. Make him work for it. Teach him what he needs to know about your body."

Nicole agreed. "That's huge! Never ever, fake it! I remember once I was dating this guy and he was a pretty good lover. I had never faked it with him, never had to. But then one night he finished quickly and seemed uninterested in helping me finish. I freaked! I became green in the face like the exorcist spewing venomous words with my head spinning around." She growled as she spoke. "You're not finished!" Nicole started shaking her head quickly with an evil look on her face. "Boy, he didn't know what to do. He panicked, then backpedaled and tried to get me back in bed, but it was too late for that. Needless to say, that relationship ended." She shrugged. "But I'm sure he'll think twice before he just leaves a girl hanging again. I mean if a guy is that thoughtless…"

Roxanne and Renee were both laughing.

"Well, I don't think I'm going to have to worry about that," Roxanne said.

"Oh, yes, you will. Trust me. You haven't had sex for a while, and he's new so it seems wonderful; well, time changes things." Renee helped herself to more broccoli. "You guys probably don't know this, but I use Nicole's guys to help create fantasies while I'm making love with Jason. You know, to spice things up. Jason has no idea, but it's fun!" She raised her eyebrows and smiled mischievously. "Jason has been the investor: Tom. He's been the naughty, nasty, tattooed biker: Stan. Jason is soon going to be a shrink." She laughed and turned to Nicole. "Has he called you yet?"

"Who?"

"My client, the psychiatrist."

"Oh, my God, that guy who called me is a shrink? He didn't leave his name or number."

Roxanne interrupted. "I don't get what you're saying. You have to fantasize to make love to your husband? That's disgusting! And you think about these lowlifes of Nicole's?"

"Ummm-humm," she said, grinning and nodding her head. "Give it five years, and you'll be living vicariously through Nicole, too."

"Excuse me! I'm sitting right here and I'm sure I'll be married within five years, and I really won't like either of you fantasizing about my husband!"

"Only flings. Husbands and boyfriends are off limits. Besides, it's not the guy. I never even met Stan. It's the type of guy. You went from a guy wearing a suit driving a Beemer, to a guy covered in tattoos riding a bike. It's a whole lot of fun!" She reached over and grabbed Nicole's arm. "It's not only you, Nicky. I use some of my client's stories, too. Like Joy, who is dating a man with a very large penis, thanks to me."

"Yeah, build it and they will come. I built it too, and they're not coming."

"What? You guys have lost me. Build what? Who's the shrink?"

"Oh, it's this guy, a client. He is a very successful psychiatrist in the area. He's single and saw the picture of the three of us. He asked if I had any single friends. I pointed to you. He asked if Nicole," she said, pointing to Nicole, "was his type. So I told him there's only one way to find out, and I gave him your number. I know we're not supposed to do that, but he's a successful shrink, and I'm sure he's not going to do anything crazy."

"Ah, no, not him." Nicole's eyes opened wide. "Me, he talks to me one time and he's going to realize I should be his client, not his date. I don't think this is a good idea."

"Why not? I think it's perfect," Roxanne said. "Besides you're supposed to be dating; we had a deal."

"I had a date. Ernie. And Frank, remember?"

"Ooh, Jason was fun that night when he was Ernie! He was a computer geek!" Renee said, winking at Nicole.

Nicole started laughing. "Fine. I'll talk to him on the phone. If I like him, we'll go on a date."

"Nicole, you've changed. You always used to be up for a date whether you liked the guy or not. Now you have to like him first?"

"You're right, something's different. I don't know, I can't put my finger on it."

"Speaking of different," Roxanne cut in. "I'm not trying to change the subject, well maybe I am, but you guys know my mom has had a weight problem her whole life."

Interested, Nicole nodded. She had always felt close to Roxanne's mom because they both struggled with weight, even though Roxanne's mom had always been at least a hundred pounds overweight, compared to Nicole's twenty or thirty.

"Well, I had the most interesting experience with my mother this morning on the phone. She confessed to me that she had eaten a whole pan of rice-crispy bars in the middle of the night. She had gotten up six times. So I started explaining to her about emotional eating, and she said that she didn't want to hear my psychobabble. Can you believe that?"

Nicole looked under the table at the skinny little Roxanne and said, "Ah, yeah. We don't want to hear about it from somebody like you. You've been skinny your whole life."

Roxanne looked at Nicole dismissively and continued. "I tried to explain that she should try to understand the reason that she keeps overeating." She took another sip of wine. "You know, she's been trying that Adkins Diet, so I said that maybe she was feeling deprived and that maybe being on that strict no-carbohydrate diet was not good for her."

Nicole rolled her eyes and glanced at Renee who was still picking at her broccoli, obviously bored with the topic. Nicole smiled, thinking that Renee was trying to figure out how to get in the teacher fantasy before Roxanne was married.

"I was trying to help her, but she was just not interested." Roxanne laughed, then said, "She told me to shut up."

Suddenly both Nicole and Renee were engrossed. Roxanne's mother had never mouthed off to anybody, especially not to her daughter.

"Anyway, she said that she liked to eat and that was that. But I…"

Nicole tried to keep a straight face when she interrupted, "Wow, I'm stuffed. Thanks for a great dinner, but do you have dessert or anything sweet to eat? Rice-crispy bars sound great!"

Renee burst out laughing. They all giggled as they got up to clear the table. They knew better than to ask for dessert at Roxanne's place. Nicole figured she had a secret fear of being fat because of her mom; she always skipped dessert. Then they all laughed again when Roxanne said she would kill for a McDonald's McFlurry.

When they were almost finished cleaning up the kitchen Roxanne asked Renee if she would like to meet Mark.

"Duh!" Renee said. "It would be nice to meet the fiancé of one of my best friends!" She turned to Nicole. "What did you think?"

"He's great, but I have one question for you, Rox." She grabbed Roxanne's shoulders and turned her toward her. "Did he sing…" In unison, Renee and Nicole sang out, "Rooooxxxanne, you don't have to turn on the red light…" They were both laughing and singing and twirling each other around in the kitchen.

"Ugh!" Roxanne despised that song and the men who sang it to her. "Mark is the only man I've met who hasn't sung that song to me. That's one reason I knew he was special."

Renee gave Nicole a strange look, then looked back at Roxanne. "Okay, we'll see."

"I'll drive," Nicole said, "but we're going to McDonald's first."

When they got to the McDonald's drive-through lane, Roxanne, who was sitting in back, said, "Tell them it's to go."

"They know."

"I know, but tell them anyway. It's funny."

"Oh, all right," Nicole said, annoyed. When she pulled up to the speaker she said, "I'd like to place an order to go."

Roxanne and Renee started laughing.

After she ordered three Oreo McFluries, she kept a straight face and said, "And now that's to go."

Nicole didn't laugh but the other two were hysterical. By the time they pulled up to the window to pay, Renee opened her door and fell out of the car with her little black dress up around her waist. She jumped up trying to pull her dress back down. She took off running into McDonald's while holding her crotch. The other two stayed in the car, laughing at Renee.

Nicole casually said to Roxanne, "Renee's friend, Joy, holds her crotch, too. Do you?"

"I don't... think so," she said, still laughing.

After they collected their McFluries they parked and waited for Renee.

Nicole turned around handing Roxanne her McFlurry and said, "You're right. That is funny."

Afterwards, the three of them intruded on Mark, and Nicole and Renee were one hundred percent certain that he was perfect for Roxanne in every way. They left Roxanne there and Nicole drove Renee home. On the drive home, Renee started talking about speed versus distance when dealing with relationships. "You travel along thinking that it's speed that matters and then one day you realize that it was never about speed, it was about distance. And you're thankful if you've made the decision to go the distance with somebody else. And it's never about looks, a great body or money in the bank; it's always about somebody compatible, somebody you can go the distance with. You stop asking how fast can I get there and you start noticing where you're going and who you're going there with."

Nicole wasn't sure if this was Jason, the mechanic, who came up with the speed and distance analogy or if it was something Renee came up with, but she liked it. She knew she had no trouble speeding into relationships, but she hoped one day she would be able to go the distance with that special one.

Chapter 14

THE NEXT MORNING Nicole woke to a FedEx delivery from her Dad. Inside were two tickets to the play her mother had wanted to see. They were a week earlier than expected, but that was fine because Nicole didn't have plans. The note said, "To my two favorite young women. I hope you are having a great weekend. I especially hope that you don't have plans tonight. Unexpectedly, I was able to get these tickets for you for your birthday. I know it's a week early but Happy Birthday, honey. I love you both."

Nicole started to cry. She knew her mother was having an affair. She didn't know what to do. She couldn't call her dad, so she called Roxanne who wasn't home and Renee who was probably still sleeping. She left a detailed message on both of their voicemails that she was sure her mother was having an affair.

Nicole grabbed her wallet and keys, and crossed the street to Starbucks crying all the while. She wondered if she might find her mother there with that Latino man she had met the night after her midlife-crisis outing. But there was no sign of her mother. When she returned home with her latte, she grabbed her cell phone and hit star-six-seven before dialing her parents' shared cell number. Praying that her mother had taken it with her so that her father wouldn't answer it and wonder why she was calling, she was prepared to hang up if he answered.

"Hello," her mother answered, with a singsong tone.

"Mom, where are you?" Nicole demanded.

"Oh, hi, honey. I'm staying with friends."

"What is going on? Where's Daddy? And where are you, geographically speaking?"

"Honey, you don't have to worry about me. I'm great. My friends and I are going to a sold-out play tonight, the one I've been dying to see."

"Mom!"

"Okay, then, goodbye." Her mother hung up the phone.

Nicole called back over and over again, but her mother had turned her phone off. Nicole's heart ached. She couldn't stop thinking about her daddy. She didn't want them to get a divorce; she didn't want him to be hurt; she just wanted to protect him.

Falling face-first onto her couch, she wept until she was emotionally exhausted.

Renee called.

"Is it my fault? I took her out. I let her play around," Nicole sobbed.

"No, Nicky, if she is having an affair, it isn't your fault. But you don't know yet. You don't know the facts," Renee sniffed.

Nicole could tell that Renee was crying, too. As tough and confident as she always was, Renee hated to see her friends hurt and vulnerable.

"Nicky, you gotta wait this one out."

"But Renee, my dad sent tickets to the play and I think she's going to the same play tonight… with him. I think I have to go and find out what's going on."

"Oh, honey, I wish I could go with you, but I can't. Jason has a party we have to go to. I could try to get out of it."

"No, don't be silly. I'm fine. I'll ask Rox, or I'll go alone. I'm fine. Maybe I should go alone anyway." Nicole's call-waiting beeped. "Oh, my call-waiting, it's Rox. Call me later." She clicked over. "Roxy."

"Tell me everything. What's going on?"

When Nicole told Roxanne everything, Roxanne agreed that she had to go to the play. Unfortunately, she had plans with Mark, so Nicole was on her own.

The three of them met later at the Starbucks by Nicole's and helped her come up with a plan. Nicole had been crying all day, and her eyes were swollen and red. Her face was splotchy and her lips looked red and chapped. She was a mess.

They were in agreement that she would go to the play. But that was as far as it went. If she ran into her mother, Nicole might find that her mother was just simply out with girlfriends. Or she might be with a man. What if she wasn't doing anything physical and it was only a male friend? They all agreed that that wouldn't be right. If her mother showed up and was with a man, Nicole's options were just to stay out of sight, avoid and witness, or confront her mother. If she were to confront her mother, what would she say? If she chose to just observe, what would she do with that information?

A man stepped next to Nicole and held a cloth that had ice inside. "Did somebody beat you up?" It was Rick.

Nicole didn't have the energy to be rude. "Sort of."

"I'm sorry. I thought maybe you would want this for your eyes." He handed it to her as Roxanne and Renee watched.

"Thanks," Nicole said and started crying again as she took the cloth.

Putting his hand on her shoulder, he said, "Let me know if there's anything I can do."

Nicole kept crying and nodded to him.

He left as Renee asked, "Who was that?"

Nicole just said, "Some guy from my building."

"That guy might like you."

"Nah, trust me. It's nothing like that."

Within the next hour, the three of them came up with a plan for every possible scenario. When Nicole got home, she was exhausted and decided to go back to bed. She hoped that when she woke up, it would all be a bad dream.

Chapter 15

NICOLE WAS DRESSED in a beautiful gold, long dress. She had bought it months ago when it was on sale and she figured someday she would want to wear a dress like that. She arrived at the theater early and took the glass elevator up to the second floor so she could look over the entrance and watch all the people coming to the play. Nicole was shaking, not from cold, but because she was upset and nervous. She waited and watched.

About fifteen minutes before the play was to begin, her mother walked in with a short Latino man. They were holding hands. As Nicole watched, the man turned to her mother and kissed her on the mouth. All the plans that Roxanne and Renee created for her went right out the window. She rushed down the stairs and grabbed her mother by the arm. Her mother's face fell and, defeated, she let go of her Latin lover and followed Nicole to a corner.

"What are you doing here?" her mother asked softly.

"Fuck you, Mother! Don't ask me that! Daddy got two tickets for us." She hit her mother's chest then her own. "For us! For your birthday!"

She was stunned by Nicole's anger. "I…"

"I'm driving you back to your husband right now! And you're going to tell him the truth!"

"I…"

"You have been using me! And lying to Daddy!" She grabbed her mother by the arm "Let's go!"

They walked by the Latino man and Nicole yelled at him, "You should be ashamed of yourself!" Shaking her finger at him. "Your relationship with my mother is over! She is married! To my father!" Then she whirled around to make sure her mom didn't communicate with him in any way.

When they got into the car her mother asked, "Where's your father? At your place?"

"No, mother, he's at home—two and a half hours away."

"You're not driving me home. My car is here!"

"You and Daddy can get it tomorrow."

Nicole's mom didn't say another word, while Nicole unloaded her anger during the drive home. "How could you do that to Dad? I mean, he loves you so much! How could you put me in that situation?" Nicole pounded on her steering wheel. "How selfish are you? You don't care about anybody but yourself." Nicole started crying again. "It's probably your fault my life is such a mess! I'm trying to find somebody as kind and loving as Daddy and here you are just shitting on a man as wonderful as him! I only wish one day I'd meet somebody who can love me as much as Daddy loves you. You don't even realize how lucky you are!" She wiped her eyes and rolled down the window for a second. "Do you even realize the situation you put me in?" The tears started rolling again. "I love you both! How can I run around trying to protect you and trying to protect him, too? How am I supposed to do that? Maybe you just don't care how I feel. Will I ever be comfortable around Daddy? Will I ever be comfortable around you again?"

She heard her mother whimper.

"You know, if you're not happy, you try to work it out, you get counseling, you talk, you work it out! I guess if you can't, you get a divorce. But you don't cheat and lie and run around on somebody who has no idea that you're not happy. You tell him, you tell somebody." Nicole stopped ranting and reached for the box of Kleenex in the backseat of her car. She wiped her eyes and embraced the silence as the car hummed down the highway.

"I'm not happy," her mother whispered and started crying harder.

Nicole had a lump in her throat and couldn't speak. She had never heard such pain and honesty from her mother. Nicole said nothing but reached out and placed her hand on her mother's leg. Her mother held on to her hand tightly. They drove home in silence, both crying.

Nicole loved her parents and she wanted them to be together. The possibility of her mother divorcing her father frightened her. When they were a few minutes from home, Nicole called her dad and woke him up. She told him that they would be there in two minutes and they needed to talk. Concerned, he said he would turn on the outside light and unlock the front door.

Nicole and her mother held hands as they walked up the front steps. Her mother turned to her and looked her in the eyes and said, "I'm sorry," and gave Nicole a hug.

Nicole waited in the living room while her mother and father went to the bedroom to talk. She sat on the couch for a while and cried, praying to God that her parents would work it out. She wanted them to stay together. As she looked at the photos on the wall, she saw many pictures of the three of them at different stages in their lives. Her family was the one constant in her life, and she didn't want to lose it.

After about an hour, her father came out and sat with Nicole in the living room. They were silent for a few minutes until he said, "Thanks for bringing her home to me." He coughed a little to avoid crying. "She said she isn't happy and she isn't sure why." He coughed again. "Thanks for bringing this to my attention. I needed to know."

"Dad, I…," she stammered and started to cry again.

"Shhh, honey, you don't have to say anything. We're all tired. Let's go to bed and we can talk in the morning."

"Daddy, I'm going home. I can't stay. You guys need to talk."

"Honey, it's late. Are you sure?"

"I'm positive. I have to go."

"Okay." He stood up and gave her a hug. "Thank you, Nicky. I love you."

"I love you, too. Is she okay?"

"She's trying to go to sleep. We're both okay, but we have a lot to talk about, decisions to make. But she'll be okay, we'll be okay." He paused, then asked, "Can I have your room for a few days?" and started to cry.

"Of course, Daddy." Nicole tried to smile through her own tears before she walked out the front door.

On the drive back to her place, Nicole stopped thinking about herself and started thinking about her mom. She had to figure out why her mother was so unhappy when she seemed to have everything a woman could want; she was a mother and a wife with a husband who loved her and gave her everything she wanted. She lived in the house she wanted, had the car she wanted to drive, the perfume she had to have and beautiful designer clothing. Nicole really didn't know what else her mother could possibly want.

She started to sob in the realization that she didn't even know her mom. She didn't know any other side of her than wife and mother. That was all she ever was to Nicole, wife and mother. She thought about everything her mother had ever done for her, and everything she had ever done for Daddy. She took care of them and loved them unconditionally. She took care of Grandpa more than Daddy did. She did for everybody around her, but what did she do for herself? Nicole tried to remember a time that her mother did something good for herself: a trip alone, a hobby she loved, even her own friends. Nicole could only come up with her mother's love for nice things.

Nicole rolled the window down to try to stop crying, but her chest was aching and almost suffocating her with tightness. Nicole was wishing her mother was beside her so she could apologize to her for not taking the time to know her. "My mommy is hurting," she sobbed out loud. She wanted the pain she felt for both her parents to stop. She started thinking about her dad who wasn't always around. He worked a lot and her mom was left alone to take care of everything. Nicole didn't remember her mother ever having a job, other than the most thankless job in life, a mother and wife.

She started thinking about what Renee had said about being selfish in a relationship with a man. She doesn't remember her mom ever being selfish until this incident. Maybe she needed a release, an escape. Maybe she didn't want to be taken for granted anymore. Nicole ached wanting to understand and hoping that her parents could work it out. She knew how much her dad loved her mom, but would it be enough?

Two and a half hours later, she was in her own bed, exhausted and confused.

Chapter 16

WHEN NICOLE WOKE up on Sunday morning and looked in the mirror, she saw a swollen and ugly face. She had a horrible headache and knew she should go back to sleep, but she knew that she wouldn't be able to so she lay in bed until Starbucks was open, thinking about everything and wishing she could go back to that first night her mother came to visit alone. Nicole should have known that there was something seriously wrong. She should have told her dad everything the next day. Maybe then her mother would have told them, or at least her dad, that she wasn't happy.

When Nicole got back home after getting her latte, Roxanne and Renee called her for a three-way talk. After five minutes on the phone they decided to come over. With another vanilla latte for Nicole and two for themselves, they settled into her living room.

"Well everything we talked about, the plans we made, I didn't remember anything. I was on auto pilot." She told them how she grabbed her mother, hit her in the chest, yelled at her and scolded her boyfriend. She told them how she drove her home, and about the things she said to her mother on that two-hour drive. "I blamed her for my messed-up life." She told them how her mother said she wasn't happy and how her dad thanked Nicole for bringing her mother home. She told them that she cried almost the whole way back home.

"Yes, I think we can tell," Renee said, getting up and giving her a hug. "I'm so sorry."

Roxanne sat dazed. "You're bringing back memories of my parent's divorce. It hurt, but I think they are happier because of it."

"Are they going to get a divorce?" Renee asked.

"I don't know. I guess now I just wait and hope that they are going to work it out."

"I really hope they work it out because your parents are the greatest."

Roxanne agreed. "Your parents have too much to let it go. I know they still love each other. They are so different than how my parents were. My parents fought all the time, all through my middle school years and half of my high school years. Well, until he moved out. Our home was so peaceful after he left."

Nicole and Renee found themselves comforting Roxanne.

"I'm sorry, but maybe it's good to think about this stuff before I get married."

"Yeah, let's talk about that. Let's talk about happy things. I've cried enough."

"Okay, well, if you want to talk about marriage stuff I have a little bit of info for you," Renee said. "And I'm not happy about it." Renee took a sip of her latte. "In marriage, after some time, we regress."

"What do you mean?" Nicole asked, giggling.

"I mean we regress back to apes or whatever. When Jason and I were in bed last night, I became aware of how we grunted to communicate. I had my computer, fashion magazines and a notebook where I was taking notes for a fashion show coming up, and he was lying on my work. Did I say, 'Honey, please get off my work?' No. I grunted, 'Un! Un!' He understood, moved and mumbled, 'Umm,' with a sorry look on his face. Have we become that lazy that we can't form sentences?"

Nicole and Roxanne were laughing. Renee's little story was exactly what Nicole needed.

"You know, you guys have treated me like I'm your little sister, like I'm not as smart as you. Well, I have news for you. I know that things aren't perfect. I know that there is no such thing as perfection in a man or a relationship. I mean, for example, Mark sometimes talks a lot. I don't know what it is, but sometimes he gets these bursts of energy usually around the time I'm winding down and getting ready for bed." Roxanne looked at

Renee. "I know that this is something that might be an issue down the road. I mean, right now it's easy because it usually happens while he's at his house and I'm at mine, so, it's only happening over the phone. The other night, I just went and made myself a turkey sandwich while he was going on and on. It wasn't a big deal."

"Wait a minute!" Renee started laughing. "Back up. You put him on speaker phone or held the phone with your shoulder while making the sandwich, right?"

"No, I was in bed and my bedside phone is corded. I just set the phone down and went and made myself a sandwich. But I was quick about it!"

Renee burst out laughing. Nicole sat with her mouth wide open and her eyes popping.

"You don't understand. Sometimes he talks a lot!"

Nicole fell sideways, laughing, and Renee took off running for the bathroom holding her crotch.

"Nicole, like once a week or every ten days, he wants to talk nonstop. He doesn't even need a grunt or an 'oh' to know I'm still there. He just simply wants to talk."

Nicole couldn't stop laughing.

"But, Nicole, I love him. I'm so madly in love with him. Everything about him, even his talking binges. I so love this man."

Still giggling, Nicole leaned over and gave her a hug.

Renee walked back into the room, saying, "Tell me again how you put the phone down and went into your kitchen to make a sandwich," and she fell on the couch laughing.

"Listen, I know that sounds bad, but the night I made the sandwich, he was reading an article to me that I wasn't interested in, so it's not as bad as it sounds. I've done little things in the past like go to the bathroom while he was talking, or go to get a bottle of water while he was talking."

"Go to the bathroom," Nicole said, picturing it and laughing.

"But what am I going to do when we live together? This makes me nervous."

Nicole and Renee sat up and tried to be serious. "Okay, okay," Nicole said between giggles.

"Honest, it's only like every ten days. But what if when I move in with him after we're married it's every night? I won't be able to go make a sandwich or go to the bathroom while he's lying next to me talking."

"Has he done it on the nights you've slept over?"

"I don't think so. I mean, we make love, and then we're both tired."

Nicole added, "If it's an article at least then you'll be able to read it yourself. Or pretend to read it." She burst out laughing again.

Renee was still laughing but managed to tell her what to do. "Okay. One of these nights, on a weekend when you don't have to get a good night's sleep, load up on coffee and make a list of things you can talk to him about. Then talk, talk your little ass off, and see how he handles it. If he says, 'Honey, I'm really tired. Can we talk about this in the morning?' then that's how you'll handle it from then on."

Nicole interrupted, "But what if he listens very intently until Roxy has nothing left to talk about? Then later, she tries to tell him that she's tired and he uses that against her, 'Remember that night? I listened to you until three in the morning. I never told you I was too tired.'"

"I see what you're saying. All I know, with Jason, if I tell him, I run the chance of becoming a nag because I usually have to tell him more than once. But if I teach him, he gets it."

"Maybe I just need to talk to him."

"Oh, that's an idea, and a mature one," Nicole said, and giggled.

"I mean, maybe it won't happen when we live together. Maybe he just misses me when I'm not with him so he tries to keep me on the phone, all hours of the night," she laughed.

Nicole got up and ran to the phone, saying "I know. Let's call the shrink!"

Renee stood up. "No, you can't do that. He's a nice guy and…"

"Why? If he's going to date me, he better learn about my crazy friends and messed up family." She began to search her caller ID for his number.

Renee stepped up to her and took the phone out of her hands. "I think we're all normal," she said, "This is life."

Nicole laughed, then said, "If you really believe we're normal, then maybe you should call him."

Chapter 17

AFTER RENEE AND Roxanne left, Nicole lay down for a nap. She felt a little better right after her friends left, but it didn't take long for reality to sink back in. She didn't know if she should call her mom or her dad or call either of them at all. Maybe she needed to give it some time.

Nicole slept for two hours and woke to a knock at her door. She looked out the peephole and saw it was her parents. *Oh, my God*, she thought as she took a deep breath and opened the door. Her parents were holding hands. Something Nicole hadn't seen in a very long time, years. They stepped in and Nicole motioned for them to join her on the couch. She didn't know what was happening; they had strange looks on their faces.

Her dad said, "I'll let the two of you have some time alone. I'll be at Starbucks across the street if you need me." He leaned over and kissed her mother on the cheek. "You okay?"

Her mother nodded.

When Nicole was alone with her mother, she started to talk. "I'm sorry I did this to you. I never meant to hurt you or your father. I'm not sure what I'm going through, but I'm going to go to a counselor; your father and I both are... I want to stay with your father, if he'll have me." She paused. "Can I have a bottle of water?"

"Yes, of course." Nicole got water for both of them.

"We've already got my car and the things I had left in, well, his place. Your father left it up to me to decide how I wanted to handle it. I had already made the decision that I wanted to save my marriage. Anyway, that went fine. Your father has been very strong."

"He loves you, Mom."

"Do you?" she asked quickly.

"Yes, I do very much."

"Was I a good mother?"

"The best, Mom, the best."

"Then why didn't you want me around?"

"Mom, I don't want to party with you. I don't want to pick up guys with you. I don't want to drink with you." Nicole stood up. "After that first night, you're right I didn't want you to come back, not the way you were." She sat back down and faced her mom. "I don't want you to be my friend, I have enough of those, and a lot of them come and go. I only have one mom—one wonderful constant in my life. I want you to be my mom." Nicole stood up again and walked by her living room window, and saw the dumpster sitting there. "I would love to go shopping, to the movies and to restaurants with you. I'd like to share my life with you, but I'd especially like you to share your life with me. Like what is your favorite perfume right now?"

"Right now, I love Givenchy Hot Couture. Thanks for asking." Her mother started to cry.

"Are you wearing it right now?"

"Yes."

Nicole sat down next to her mother and gently took her hand to smell her wrist. "I love it."

"Thank you. I want to be noticed, somebody to be interested in me, to feel like I matter." She took her hand back from Nicole. "I've allowed myself to slip into a rut, a rut of mother and wife with nothing special to offer."

"Oh, Mom, you have so much to offer. I know there's so much I still need to learn from you."

"Nicole, I'm not trying to blame you or your father. I made this mess, and the beginnings of this mess started a long time ago. I allowed myself to fall into a rut, to lose track of my needs in my life. I just hope that you and your father will stick with me while I sort it all out."

"You're my one and only mom and the only mom I would ever want. I'm sticking with you. And I'm really glad that you are going to try to make it work with Daddy."

"Speaking of Daddy, I'm going to go and get him. He'd like to talk to you alone, too." They stood up and hugged each other for a long time, neither wanting to let go.

About five minutes later, her father knocked on the door and walked in. Nicole's first thought was, *Oh, my God, he's left Mom alone in Starbucks and she might meet somebody.* Then she calmed herself down by telling herself, *Mom said she wanted to work it out with Dad.*

"Hi, honey." He sat down in the chair facing her. "We've been talking all day, and we have decided to try to make it work. We may both go through some changes, which could be good for both of us. I hope we stay together. I love your mother very much." He put his hands together as if praying and Nicole knew his fatherly guidance was coming. "If you need to talk, we are here for you, and we will be open with you. But as far as you holding guilt, or feeling like you did something wrong, you didn't; your mother and I did." He turned to look at Nicole. "I know you have been dragged into this, and I'm thankful you did what you did; so is your mother. But from this day forward, this has nothing to do with you and, frankly, it is none of your business. I'm letting you off the hook."

Nicole started to cry. She hadn't known she needed to be released, but she did and she needed to hear those words.

"Please don't think less of her or love us less, Nicky. We're human." He stood up and pulled Nicole up beside him. They hugged. Nicole knew she needed to help her mom feel better by showing her how much she appreciated her and didn't take her for granted. After giving her parents some time to heal, she would go home to visit more often. She missed her mom.

Nicole said her good-byes to her parents, then headed to the gym to read her book while she rode the stationary bike. She had a hard time concentrating on her book, because she couldn't stop thinking about her parents. Her parents had let her off the hook, but she had to let herself off the hook, too.

Rick stepped into the gym wearing shorts and a t-shirt.

"Oh, my God. Does anybody else use this gym, or just you?"

"And you," he said, sitting down on the bench. "Are you okay?"

"Yes, I'm fine. I've just had a rough weekend."

"Did you break up with your mean boyfriend?"

Nicole started laughing. "That's funny."

He smiled and winked at Nicole.

Nicole's heart started to race, hating that she was attracted to him. *When did this happen? When did he go from being Rick the Dick to Rick the Dick?* Oh, how she wanted to sneak a peak, and take a good hard look at his crotch. Every time she was around him, she just wanted to see what he was packing, not that she'd be able to tell anything. Thinking about him and trying to avoid looking at *it* caused her to break out in a sweat, so she decided it was best to go home and take a cold shower. Maybe she would enjoy the company of her vibrator before going to sleep early.

When Nicole got home she jumped in the shower, her first shower of the day. She felt something under her left arm, a small bump. She rubbed her other armpit and it didn't feel the same. Panicking, she pressed against the lump with her fingertips. It was tender. Moaning, "Oh, no," she quickly rinsed off, stepped out of the shower and dried herself. When she looked at her armpit in the mirror, she couldn't see the lump. She took a deep breath and tried to relax. She got into her pajamas and decided to skip the rendez-vous with her vibrator. The lump had banished the thought of sex from her mind.

She went into the kitchen and made herself a bowl of Fruity Pebbles, then went into the living room and turned on the TV. Maybe she was just overtired and stressed. Maybe a good night's sleep would fix everything. Shoveling down her cereal, she tried to forget about her lump.

When she was finished eating and had taken the bowl to the kitchen, she went back onto the bathroom and took off her pajama top. She felt for the lump and realized the area was getting more tender. No longer thinking it was cancer, she was starting to believe that her glands were swollen. But she had no infection that would cause her glands to swell—unless she had an internal infection or she did have cancer. She couldn't relax until she found out what was causing the swelling and tenderness, so she called Renee to take her to the emergency room. It was Sunday night, Renee's

Saturday night, because she rarely worked on Mondays. Renee said she would be right over.

Nicole couldn't stop thinking about the worst-case scenario. Tired and depressed and because the way her life was going, she wouldn't be surprised if she... she stopped herself. She didn't want to think about having cancer. On the drive to the hospital, Renee kept her hand on Nicole's leg. "How much does one person have to go through?" Renee said.

Renee dropped Nicole off at the emergency room entrance and went to park the car. When Nicole went inside, she was surprised that nobody was in the waiting room. "Wow, it's a quiet night."

"For the moment. What's the problem?"

"I have a lump under my arm."

Renee came up beside her, and started to rub Nicole's back.

"I need you to fill this out." The nurse handed her a clipboard with papers. "And I need your insurance card."

Nicole had her card ready and gave it to the nurse as she stared to fill out the paperwork.

"You know what, we're going to take you back right now. You can finish filling that out later. Follow me," the nurse said.

Nicole and Renee followed her into the examining room. "Take off everything above your waist and put on this gown. When you're ready have a seat on the table. The doctor will be right in, and I'll be back for the clipboard."

Renee sat on one of the chairs, and Nicole took off her shirt but left her bra on. "I'm not taking my bra off, not yet." She put the gown on, sat on the table and finished filling out the forms. When the nurse came back, she checked Nicole's temperature and blood pressure. "It shouldn't be long now," she said and left again.

Within a couple of minutes, a dark-haired, handsome doctor walked in whistling. "Hello there," he said, then turned to greet Renee. He glanced at the folder with Nicole's information and said, "Your temp and blood pressure is good. Good. Okay, so you have a lump under your left arm. Let's take a look."

Nicole looked at Renee and raised her eyebrows and grinned because she thought he was cute. The gown was loose enough that she didn't have to remove it, but she was embarrassed that he had to look at her armpit. Nicole lifted her left arm while fanaticizing that this doctor would save her life and later realize that he had fallen in love with her. They would marry and live happily ever after.

Her dream was overtaken by pain as he pressed against her lump. It was sore and she was scared. "Oh, that's it right there. I can feel it. It hurts," Nicole said, because she didn't want him pushing any harder.

"Okay." He moved his head a little closer and said, "Okay," again.

Nicole was trying to read his okays. Did that okay mean yes, it's a swollen lymph gland, or it's something worse.

"Okay, Nicole," he said, writing in his notebook, "you have an ingrown hair."

Renee started to laugh. But Nicole ignored her. "What? Are you sure?" she stammered.

"Yes, I'm sure," he said, and continued writing in her file.

Nicole gave Renee a dirty look.

"No, I didn't mean anything, Nicole. That's wonderful news."

"Yeah, you're right, but I'm still humiliated." She asked the doctor, "Are you sure? Should you take another look?"

"No, I'm sure."

"I'm sorry I wasted your time."

The doctor kept a straight face and stayed in control. He was also kind enough to write out a prescription to make it sound more serious. "This should take care of it," handing her the prescription.

Nicole took it, smiling dejectedly. "I had a rough weekend."

"Well then, I hope this news makes it better. It's nothing serious."

"Well, it has and it hasn't."

He put his hand on her thigh and gave it a little squeeze, asking. "Is there anything else I can help you with tonight?"

"Wait a minute, wait a minute, I'm thinking." She stood up and looked her body over. "Renee, is there anything else wrong with me?" She coughed, checking to see if she had a cold. "Have I complained about anything else lately? I mean this ingrown hair is going to cost me about five hundred bucks, my deductable."

Renee started laughing again. "Well, Doctor, maybe you could check her hum-hum," she said as she looked at Nicole's crotch.

Nicole closed her eyes. "Thank you, Renee. If I wasn't humiliated enough…" she said, giving Renee a dirty look, then asked the doctor, "Could you prescribe me some drugs, so I don't have to feel all of this humiliation?"

He didn't even smile.

"No, I guess that's it," Nicole said, while taking off her gown.

The doctor left and Nicole put her top back on. "Renee, don't tell anybody. This is just between you, me, the doctor and my insurance company, okay?" They walked to the front counter to get her papers and insurance card. As they were leaving, Renee saw one of her clients, a doctor who worked at that hospital.

"Hi, Renee. What are you doing here? Are you okay?"

"Yes, my friend here, Nicole, had a lump, but it's fine. How are you?"

"Oh, you're the one, an ingrown hair, right?" She giggled pleasantly and rested her hand on Nicole's forearm.

"Good news travels fast. I'm sure everybody needed a good laugh on this quiet Sunday night," Nicole said, trying to be funny but sounding sarcastic.

"Trust me, it's better to put your mind at ease. And we've had much less interesting cases than yours." She smiled warmly at Nicole. "Oh, did you hear about the guy who went to see his doctor because everything hurt. He pointed to his chin and said ouch, he touched his leg and said ouch, he touched his arm and said ouch. The doctor said, 'You have a broken finger.'"

Nicole smiled, pretending to think it was funny.

"A little doctor humor; I couldn't resist." She turned back to Renee. "I love my hair. You did an outstanding job on my color."

"Well, you look great."

"Thanks. Hey, I better get back, I have a patient waiting. Ciao."

"Yeah, I plan to," Nicole said under her breath as the two headed out of the hospital. "Take me to the nearest Taco Bell. They're still open, right?"

"Yes, they're open but I'm not taking you. You've been doing so good with your exercising, and you would be mad at yourself if you pigged out. Nicky, you just need a good night's sleep, so I'm going to take you home."

"You're right, I'm not hungry. I'm humiliated."

"Why?" She started her car. "Okay, Nicole, I'm going to tell you something that you can't tell anybody. Promise?"

"I promise."

"Jason rushed me to the hospital about two months ago because I thought I was having a miscarriage, but I was just having my period. There, I hope you feel better."

Nicole started laughing. "I do feel better. But when did this happen? I didn't know you were trying to have a baby?"

"Trust me, we're not!" She turned on her blinker and merged onto the highway. "I really thought I was pregnant. I felt the baby kicking and everything. God, I even made Jason feel." She started laughing. "Nicole, a baby isn't kicking at one month. I was a lunatic! I'm not sure what I was going through, but it was crazy. I had looked at the wrong calendar. I have my work calendar and my personal calendar and for some reason I went back two months and didn't see my little red heart, the mark I put on my calendar when I get my period."

"You put a heart? I put the devil, with horns, although last month I put a great big smiley face. I'm sorry, continue."

"And my body felt different. I was cramping more and craving barbeque sauce. Jason loved that. I cried more, too; I cried because I didn't want a baby, and I cried because maybe I did. Maybe I wanted one and thought we were ready for a baby." She turned to Nicole. "Do you think I want to have a baby?"

"I don't know. How did you feel when you learned that you weren't pregnant?"

"I felt relieved, with just a touch of sadness. Nicole, I was feeling this baby kick, which was probably just gas." She started laughing. "Gas, Nicole! I was very attached to my gas!"

Nicole joined in laughing. "Thanks for cheering me up!"

"Nicole, do I want to have a baby? I'm serious. Do I?"

"Yes, Renee, I think you do."

"I think I do, too. You know, I think Jason might be ready himself. He was so gentle with me. I was mortified after we left the hospital. I couldn't say sorry enough. But now," she said, rolling her eyes, "I'm the butt of his jokes. His latest one is, 'Renee! Come here quick! You gotta feel this!' He'll place my hand on his stomach and tell me the baby's kicking, then he'll let out a big, loud fart."

Nicole burst out laughing. "That is good!"

"Yeah, it's funny." Renee pulled up to Nicole's building and put the car in park. "I guess I need to have a talk with Jason to see if he's ready. I know I don't want one this year, but maybe next year we should start trying. I'll talk to him, and I'll let you know."

Nicole's eyes filled with tears. "You know, this is very exciting and I'm really happy for you." She opened the car door. "I'll start thinking of good names—like Nicole for a girl." She reached over and gave Renee a hug. "Thanks for taking me to the hospital and for cheering me up."

"I love you, Nicky. And thanks for cheering me up. We now each have our hospital stories."

Nicole laughed, closed the car door and walked into her condo building. But the laughter quickly turned to tears because she felt worn out and stupid because of her ingrown hair. One best friend was getting married and now the other was having a baby. Nicole's parents were on shaky ground, and she still blamed herself for her mother's affair.

Nicole's heart ached, thinking that Renee had Jason to take her to the hospital, to be with her when she was scared, and Nicole was alone. And soon, Renee wouldn't be there, either; she would be busy with a baby, and Roxanne would be busy with her new husband. Nicole climbed the stairs with tears rolling down her cheeks. She dreaded walking into her empty condo, so she stood outside her door and cried. It was late, almost midnight, and she knew she would have a busy day at work, but she couldn't find the strength to open her door and go inside. She stood there, leaning her forehead against the door.

Suddenly, Rick was standing next to her, looking half asleep and saying, "What are you doing?"

"Oh. I'm sorry, did I wake you?"

"You were moaning."

Nicole started laughing. "I was not!" she said, trying to stop laughing. "No, I wasn't."

"Yes, you were. Why else would I be standing here in the middle of the night? What is wrong with you?"

"Nu…thing!" Nicole was laughing so hard she couldn't catch her breath.

"Yes, there is something wrong, and I'm taking you out for dinner tomorrow night so we can get to the bottom of it!" He turned to walk away. "Goodnight, Nicole," he said, then turned back, took her keys and unlocked her door. He opened her door and turned on her lights. "Please go to sleep."

Nicole pouted while staring at her opened door.

"Are you okay?"

Nicole suddenly had a brilliant idea: sex with Rick the *Dick*. That was the one thing that would make her feel better. "You're right, I'm not doing very good. Could you help me to my bedroom?"

"Sure." He wrapped his arm around her and helped her to her room. He helped her sit on the bed. "You're okay now, right?"

"Could you help me take off my shirt?"

"No. Nicole, I can't," he said laughing nervously.

"Why-eee?" she asked, pouting.

"Nicole, I'll be at your door at seven tomorrow night to go out for dinner. I'm leaving now, so lock your door behind me."

"Okay." She stood up and followed him to the door. "Thanks for helping me inside."

"You're welcome, Nicole. Get some sleep."

"I will," she said, and closed and locked her door. Nicole set her alarm, fell into bed and was fast asleep within seconds.

Chapter 18

THE NEXT DAY at work, Nicole thought she remembered asking Rick to have dinner with her, so she called his office to cancel. "Hi, I'm not sure why I asked you to have dinner with me, but I didn't mean it. I'm not a glutton for punishment, at least I don't think I am, maybe I am, I don't know. But I do know that you like to laugh at me, and I cannot have dinner with somebody who makes fun of me and laughs at me. So I'm cancelling our dinner plans, that is, if we had dinner plans."

Nicole knew how foolish that message sounded, but she didn't care anymore when it came to Rick. She only wished he would have slept with her last night because for once she might have enjoyed his company. And maybe with any luck, he never would have talked to her again.

Nicole also realized she needed one more treatment of laser hair removal. After two treatments, she thought she wouldn't need anymore because of her light hair. But the ingrown hair under her arm was a clear sign that she still needed more treatments. Nicole scheduled an appointment for right after work.

When she got to the medical spa a block from her bank, she checked in and was told to have a seat in the waiting room. She picked up a magazine and sat down. Nicole was alone in the waiting room until a woman with a baby stroller came in and sat down on the couch across from Nicole. She said to the baby, "You must be hungry."

Oh, God, no. Please no, she thought, hoping that the woman wouldn't try to breast feed. Sure enough, the woman pulled out her breast and stuck the baby on it. Nicole didn't look, even though she wanted to. Her uneasiness made her want to blurt out, "That's handy," or "I sure am thirsty," but instead, she tried to keep from laughing. One moment, she thought it was cool, the loving bond between mother and child, but the next moment, she was so uncomfortable that she couldn't stop thinking of funny things to say and struggled to not laugh out loud.

When the woman said, "Are you going to eat or just play on it?" Nicole couldn't control herself. Laughter welled up in her throat, and she had to run to the bathroom so she could let loose. She knew she was being rude but she couldn't help it. Then she wondered if she was so nervous because of Renee wanting to have a baby. She decided to call her and left a message. "Renee, when you have a baby, please don't be obnoxious about breastfeeding it in public. I'm in the bathroom right now because I am so uncomfortable about this woman who wants the world to know she's breastfeeding her baby. I'll buy you those cover-up blankets for your baby shower."

A woman came into the bathroom, so Nicole went into a stall and whispered, "Listen, this woman exposed her breast like it was her arm. I don't like that, Renee. I don't like that at all. I don't want you or Rox doing that. I know I'm being bossy, but please consider our feelings, the feelings of the childless and husbandless. Oh, and FYI, I'm at the med-spa for hopefully my last underarm hair removal treatment. Call me later."

Nicole left a similar message on Roxanne's voicemail, then went back to the waiting room hoping that milk jugs wouldn't be there. She wasn't. Nicole relaxed with her magazine until she was called back for her laser treatment: bikini line and underarms.

When Nicole got home around six-thirty, she had a message on her home phone. "Hi, Nicole, it's Rick." He was laughing. "Nicole, you didn't ask me out for dinner, I asked you." He laughed some more. "Anyway…"

Nicole deleted the message before he finished. She didn't want to hear it and she wanted to have sex with him more than ever, even though she couldn't stand him. As she got into her pajamas, she could smell the dumpster, so she grabbed the can of spray and opened the bedroom window. She directed the spray right at the dumpster, emptying the can, then throwing it in with the rest of the garbage. She closed the window and the blind. She heard somebody knock at her door, she looked through the peephole and saw Rick standing there. She opened the door, saying, "Hi, I can't have dinner with you."

"Yes, I know, you left me a message. Did you get my message that I was going to stop by to check on you and if you wanted to talk…"

"Oh, I…"

"Have you eaten?"

"No, I…"

"Nicole, I'm just going to say it. I'd like to get to know you. Since you've been at this building, since I've met you, I've found myself very entertained by you. I look forward to seeing you, just seeing you, makes me smile. And I'm not sure why you have this effect on me, but I would like to investigate it. I'm under the impression that you are single. Is that right?"

"Yes, I'm single, but now I have to be honest. Every time I see you, I feel humiliated, embarrassed. I think," she said, pointing at his chest, touching his firm muscle, which made her heart pound because she hadn't expected him to be so hard, "that you think I'm a fool. And I'm not a fool, okay?"

"Nicole, do you want to go with me to get a bite to eat, or not?"

"Yes, let me grab my bag." She didn't realize until they were in the car that she was in her pajamas, a yellow t-shirt and white flannel bottoms with little yellow bunnies on them. "Do you see what I'm talking about," she groaned. "I can't go eat with you, I'm in my pajamas! Why did you let me leave the house like this?"

"Nicole, you look great to me. Let's get drive through and eat in the car. We can park over by the airport and watch the planes land."

"Okay, that sounds nice. I haven't been there for a long time. I used to work at a bank by the airport, and I'd pick up Chinese and sit there and eat lunch while planes came and went."

"Let's do that."

He ran in to get the menus while she waited in the car. He brought out the menus along with two Diet Cokes, took her order of steamed veggies and honey chicken, and he went back inside to place the order. Nicole found Rick easy to be around; she liked him, but didn't know if she liked him more as a friend than a lover. She didn't know if there was that spark for either of them.

Nicole was having one of the nicest evenings she had had in a long time. She confessed that she had been crying because her parents were going through some hard times, sparing him the details. He told her that his mother was well and living in Arizona, and that his father had passed away a year ago. Nicole wanted to ask him his age but didn't dare because he described his parents as if they were older, she figured he must be older than her.

When they finished eating, they got out of the car to throw away their Chinese food containers in a nearby dumpster. Before getting back in, a police car pulled up behind them, blocking their car's exit. The officer got out and asked them both for ID and why they were in the area. It sounded like Rick was going to mouth off to the cop and get them both into trouble. "I'm on a date. What, are ya blind?"

The cop aggressively walked up to Rick.

"How's it going man?" Rick said, grabbing the officer's hand, then executing a quick, manly embrace. "I haven't seen you since we played in Atlanta. How's the wife?"

"Rick, man, Steph is great. We're getting ready to have our first baby, a son."

"Congratulations, that's awesome! What are you doing, man? You're a cop? You hate cops!" He laughed and gave him a nudge. "Man, it's been too long. We gotta get together." He turned toward Nicole.

"Nicole, this is my long-lost friend, Bud. We used to play ball together." He placed his hand on Nicole's shoulder. "This is Nicole my soon-to-be girlfriend." He looked at Bud, then said, "We're not quite there yet. I'm working on it."

Bud laughed and shook Nicole's hand. "Nice to meet you, Nicole. And I don't know if this will help, but he's a great guy."

Rick laughed. "Thanks, man."

"Hey, I did my part."

"What's up, chasing people out of here?"

"New curfew around here, a lot of crime in the area. In fact, I want you to head out. A lot of punks around here lookin' for trouble, especially at night."

"You got it," Rick said. "You ready?" he asked Nicole.

Bud gave Rick his card. "Give me a call. You gotta see Steph. We were just talking about you the other day."

Bud gave Rick another quick hug and watched Rick get into his car.

Nicole waved to say goodbye to Bud, then locked her car door.

"It's so great to run into old friends. It's easy to get busy with life."

Nicole turned toward him and said, "You know, you are kind of nice. I thought you were not so nice. Thanks for taking me out, even in my pajamas. I had a really good time."

"Thanks for coming with me and giving me a chance."

When Nicole got home, she had three messages on her phone: one from Renee, one from Roxanne and one from the shrink.

Nicole called Renee.

"I promise I won't breastfeed my baby obnoxiously!"

Nicole started laughing. "Thank you, Renee. Now I need your advice. Your shrink called me again, but I just don't know if I want to date anybody right now."

"Nicole, maybe you do need a shrink," she said, laughing. "Call him and tell him you're not interested then, in the nicest possible way, of course. Nicole, it's not that difficult."

"Okay, you're right. I just don't think a shrink would be a good fit for me. I think he would analyze me all the time."

"That's an excuse, Nicole. You haven't even talked to him. You don't even know him."

"You know, I gotta go. I… I'm going to call him."

"Okay, call me back."

"Okay."

Nicole dialed his number and he answered. After the hellos, he said, "Hey, I was wondering if you would be interested in meeting me for a drink one evening this week. So we can meet in person." They agreed to meet on Thursday after work at a little bar a block from Nicole's bank. Twenty minutes later, Nicole hung up the phone and went to bed.

Chapter 19

HER THURSDAY NIGHT drink date was nice, but she knew she only wanted the shrink as a friend. Driving home, she was bluntly honest with herself, admitting that there was no way she could or would be attracted to any other man because she was so strongly drawn to Rick. She hated to admit the attraction because he had been the person she despised for the last few months. She couldn't stop thinking about him and how easy he was to be around on Monday night when they parked and ate Chinese. He made her feel important and pretty even though she was in her pajamas.

When Nicole got back to her condo, she checked her mail. The other woman who regularly attended the condo meetings was also checking her mail. Seeing Nicole, she said, "I wish I had left when you did. They ran out of time and didn't even allow me to ask my one question. The president told me to write it down and drop it in the comments box in the office."

"You're kidding me!"

"I guess you don't have to go through the same channels as the rest of us now that you're dating the owner."

"What? No, I'm not dating anybody."

"I saw you get into his car with him on Monday night. You looked pretty comfortable together."

"Oh, no. I just went for a bite to eat with Rick, the manager."

"Rick's the owner. Well, not of our building, but he owns the east building. He used to own this building, but he fixed it up and sold it off as

condos, our condos, but that building," she said, pointing. "The east building is apartments."

"No, I don't think so. Rick's the manager of the building." Nicole
locked her mailbox. "Well, it was nice seeing you again. Maybe I'll see you
at the next meeting, and we can stir up some trouble."

"That sounds like fun. Let's do it!"

Nicole decided to brush her off. She sounded like a nosey neighbor
who didn't have the facts. She hoped she wouldn't spread anything around
about Rick and her going out.

She went up to her condo and called the shrink. When he answered,
she said, "Hi, it's Nicole. I just wanted to say that I had a nice time tonight,
but I'm in a strange place, trying to sort some stuff out, and I really don't
want to date anybody right now. I need to work through some things."

"I sensed that you had a lot on your mind, Nicole. Don't worry about
it; I understand. If you find yourself in a better place and you're interested,
give me a call."

"Thank you. I'll keep your phone number, and thanks for under-
standing."

When she hung up, she knew that she would keep his phone number.
He was a nice guy and he was attractive, but Nicole had to find out how she
felt about Rick before she could move forward. There was a knock at
Nicole's door. It was Rick.

"Hi, Nicole. I just wanted to say that I had a nice time with you
Monday night, and I hope we can do it again sometime soon."

"That would be nice. You were great company."

"Oh, and I wanted to tell you that the dumpster should be out of here
by next month."

"Why... I mean, that's great, but what happened?"

"The president made a decision. And the decision was to get moving
on a few things that have been a problem for the building and the owners."

"Oh, speaking of owners. I'm not trying to spread rumors, but somebody told me that you used to own this building and that you own the east
building."

"Well, my company owns the building. It was my father's company, and before he passed away, I became involved. He left it all to me. So, yes, in a roundabout way, it is my building."

"Oh." Nicole didn't know what to say, surprised that it was true and even more surprised that he seemed to want to talk about it. So she invited him in.

"Nicole, between you and me, it was the best move I've ever made. My father and I didn't get along for years. I wanted to play pro ball, baseball, and he wanted me to be involved in his business. After failing miserably in sports, I made up with my dad and the last few years of his life, he was my best friend. Not making the pros was the best thing that ever happened to me."

Nicole went to the refrigerator for two bottles of water, then she joined him on the couch. "Wow, tough lessons with a nice ending. Well, and a sad ending. How did your father die?" She leaned against the armrest facing him, not far from him because he was sitting in the center of the couch.

Rick turned to face her. "My dad smoked his whole life and died of emphysema. He'd been on oxygen the last couple years of his life." He took a drink of water. "He was older and had a good life. My parents had me when they were older than most. My dad was seventy-nine when he died, and my mom's about ten years younger than him. She's still very well and happy living in Arizona. The dry air suits her. Me, I like a little humidity."

"I do, too. I love humidity and especially how warm it always feels at night. When I moved here I was so happy about the climate. It felt like a Minnesota summer all year long."

"It's kind of funny, my mom is undefeated in go-kart racing."

Nicole didn't believe him. "No way."

"Yeah, she belongs to some club. She's in a retirement community. And what's even funnier is that my mom never had her driver's license until a couple of years before my dad died. I thought she didn't want to drive, I thought she was scared."

"Are you kidding me?"

"No, I'm serious. My mom has taught me a lot in the last couple of years. Her life always revolved around me and my dad, but now her life revolves around her. I've never seen her happier. I've tried to get her to move back, so I can keep an eye on her but she tells me she's too busy… and never lonely. She says her dance card is always full." He grinned. "I'm not exactly sure what that means, and I don't think I want to know."

Nicole watched him. She liked the mellow tone of his voice. She liked the way he sometimes talked with his hands. She liked how his lip curled slightly at times. She liked how comfortable he looked on her couch. But most of all, she liked that she was falling for him.

"I don't think my dad meant to hold her back in anyway, he wasn't that kind of guy, but I think he did and I see her today, so full of joy; I wish she had always had that." He took a drink of his water. "She swears she wouldn't change a thing. But it makes me think… never want to hold a woman back."

Nicole looked at him sideways. "What are you trying to do? Seduce me?"

"Is it working?"

"No."

"Well, it was worth a shot." He tapped her leg. "So, Nicole, have you talked to your parents?"

"No, I have made a vow to stay out of it. I think they need some time without me. I'll let them call me when they want to." Nicole looked into Rick's eyes, and neither looked away. "So how do you like your dad's business?"

"Well, I never would have believed it, but I love it more than I ever loved baseball." He chuckled.

"You're kidding me?" she said, giggling.

"No, but I've found a way to integrate everything I learned in sports into this business, and it has been a winning combination. I learned about team work and discipline from sports, and I learned about business and people skills from my father."

"People skills? I didn't know you had any," she teased.

Rick leaned in and kissed Nicole.

Nicole let him kiss her, but she didn't kiss him back. She wanted to find out what he would do. His kiss was soft, but she sensed that his entire body was hard with desire for her.

He sat back up and continued talking. "Now, I'm trying to decide if I want to do the same thing to the east building that I've done to this building. I have a lot to think about. I'm also looking to purchase another building not far from here. It's smaller, but it has good bones. It's a solid building and a good location."

Nicole glanced at his groin area. She couldn't help herself. She thought she could see some expansion in his pants, but she wasn't sure; she had nothing to compare it to because she had never been brave enough to look before.

He noticed her looking and kissed her again. This time, she kissed him back. Nicole's eyes were still closed when she said, "Okay, Rick. You have to go now." She stood up and grabbed his hands to help him up and lead him out of her condo.

"Don't you want me to help you take off your shirt?" He laughed as he followed her to the door.

Nicole laughed, too, and opened her door, giving him a gentle shove out.

"Just one more," he said, and leaned toward her.

"No." She laughed and stepped back. "You have to go."

"Would you like to have dinner with me Wednesday night at my place? I'll cook."

"I'd love to. What time?" She gave him another little shove so she could close her door.

"Is seven okay?"

"Perfect." She closed and locked the door. When Nicole walked into her bedroom, she was still smiling. She got into her pajamas and opened the blinds to look outside at the dumpster. It had always been a little junky in the alley, but since the dumpster moved in, it had gotten worse. There was enough space for five or six cars to park back there, but instead it seemed to be a muddy storage space for a few bicycles, a shopping cart, a couple of empty pallets, a wooden crate and a lot of garbage, some inside the dumpster and some that didn't make it into the dumpster.

It was almost dark out. She sat on the window sill and her eyes started to fill up with tears. She didn't know why. Maybe she had grown attached to that stinky garbage bin. Or maybe it was something it represented. Sitting there crying, trying to sort out her feelings, she heard something and looked over at Rick's window. He waved, then opened his window. "You okay?"

He wasn't wearing his shirt, but she couldn't get a good look, only a shadowy silhouette. "Yes," she said and wiped her eyes, "Just saying good-bye to the dumpster." She laughed nervously, then started crying again.

"Anything I can do?"

"I could use some lovin'," she said and smiled at Rick.

"I'll be right over."

Nicole laughed and wiped her eyes again. "I don't know, Rick. I think I'm happy."

"Really?"

"Yes, really. I really like my life. I mean, I have my share of struggles. I have my ups and downs, but I really love my life."

"That's wonderful, Nicole. I'm pretty happy, too." Rick leaned a little too far out his window and lost his balance. His body fell forward and his legs kicked up and got tangled in his blind string. His arm anchored against the side of the wall kept him from falling. The blinds fell down and hit his head before falling to the floor.

Nicole stood up quickly and bumped her head on her window. "Oh, my God! Are you okay?" She held her head in pain.

Rick, barely acknowledging that he had almost fallen out his window, was more concerned about her bumping her head. "Are you okay?"

"I'm okay. Are you okay?"

"Yes, I'm okay."

"What just happened?"

"Well, I think I almost fell out my window. This could be dangerous, so you wanna come over?"

Nicole laughed. "I'd love to, Rick, but that could be dangerous, too. I wouldn't be able to control myself, so I'm going to stay right here."

"Are you sure? I promise I won't touch you. I won't kiss you."

"What if I can't make that same promise?"

"You don't have to. I have no problem moving things along. Why postpone the inevitable? Ten years from now we'll still be kicking ourselves for not being quicker about it."

"Yeah, I think I've heard that line before. Goodnight, Rick."

"Nicole, it's not a line. Wait, what do you want for dinner?"

"Um, how about spaghetti?"

"That's an easy one."

"Exactly. I don't know if you can cook."

Rick laughed as he stepped back to close the window.

Nicole closed her window and her blinds before she got into bed. She had a very necessary date with her vibrator.

Chapter 20

THE NEXT DAY at work, Nicole decided to screw giving her parents time, and she called her mom. "Mom, what are you doing tomorrow? Because it's going to be a beautiful day and I thought maybe we could go spend the day at the beach. Remember when we used to spend the day at the lake in Cannon Falls?"

Her mother agreed to make the trip but couldn't come until morning, which worked perfectly. She arrived about ten-thirty and Nicole had her beach towels, sunglasses and sunscreen ready to go. She was really looking forward to a day with her mom.

They came up with the great idea to buy their way into one of the fancy hotels so they could use their facilities: valet parking, restaurant, bathrooms, pool, lounge chairs, towels and umbrellas, which Nicole with her fair skin would probably need. Two handsome young men set up their chairs and umbrella after receiving a generous tip from her mother. "We'll get good service now. I think this beats Cannon Falls." She smiled and nudged Nicole. She turned to the young men and asked, "Could we get some menus, too?"

Nicole and her mom got comfortable on the luxurious lounge chairs and Nicole slopped on the sunscreen. "I hope I can get a little color without burning." Nicole glanced at her mom and thought she fit right in with the rich and fancy people in South Miami. She made a mental note: *Not only does Mom like nice things, she fits in to that lifestyle, it suits her.*

A server came over to take their drink order and they both ordered a virgin Miami Vice. Nicole turned to her side facing her mom. "Mom, what did you like to do when you were little, I mean, before you met Daddy?"

"Wow, now you're taking me back." She put her hand to her chin and looked up. "Well," she seemed to choke up a little. "I loved hanging out with my dad on the tractor in the fields."

Nicole didn't see that coming. "Really?" she said chuckling. "Really?"

"Yes, I liked the smell, a mixture of gasoline, Dad's sweat and the fresh-cut hay."

"How come I never knew that?" She made another mental note: *Mom likes a lot of smells, not just expensive perfume.* "What else did you like?"

"I was a tomboy," she said, almost startling herself. "Yeah, I was a tomboy. I used to climb trees, catch turtles and snakes and tip cows. But what I loved most was jumping on horses." Her face started to glow. "Nicole, my friends, we used to search out pastures with horses, and ride them. We'd just jump on, no saddle, no bridle, sometimes no halter. Often the horses were tame but sometimes they weren't, and then we'd have the ride of our lives."

"I can't picture it."

"See this scar? I got it from one horse, Cracker." She laughed. "I was the only one who dared get on him. Oh, did he take me for a ride!" She pointed back to her leg. "He threw me off against a barbed wire and electric fence. The barb caught me here, and I got twelve stitches and a reputation." She brushed off her scar like she could make it go away. "That was fun, a good memory."

"Tell me more. What else did you do?"

The server came back with the menus and their slushy drinks. Her mom ordered tuna and Nicole ordered a turkey and avocado sandwich; both opted for the fruit instead of the fries as a side.

"You're making healthier choices. Very nice, and it's showing."

"Thanks, Mom. That means a lot to me." Nicole took a quick scan of her body and felt pretty good about herself. "Mom, what happened? I mean, what changed? How did you go from tomboy to elegant woman?"

"You know, Nicole, it's funny you should ask. I'm trying to sort some things out with my counselor, and that question is parallel to what I'm working on." She took a sip from her drink. "I think I had some ideas about what a wife and mother should be, and I tried to become that, maybe losing myself in the process. I do know that when your father started making more money, I felt even more pressure to be the perfect wife because, after all, he was the perfect husband. Well, and then we moved to Naples, I mean it's no Miami, but it's nice. We live in a beautiful area. I think I got swallowed up. Don't get me wrong, I love all of it, but sometimes I still feel so very out of place, which makes me try even harder to keep up with what I think I should be."

"What you think you should be or what other people think you should be?"

"I'm not sure. I don't think your dad puts any pressure on me to be something, and I've never felt pressure from you either. It's either strangers or myself."

"What does it mean if it's you doing that to yourself?"

"I'm not sure. It's something I'll have to figure out. But I think, if that's the case it could have something to do with self-esteem."

"Ah, that good old self-esteem." She held up her glass. "Let's toast to self-esteem!"

"Okay." Her mom held up her glass. "Cheers to self-esteem."

"And may we both always have tons of it."

When their sandwiches came, Nicole's mom kept the tip money flowing.

Nicole had an idea. "Do you think we should see if we can get in for facials or massages at the spa?"

"Yes, let's," she said with a mischievous smile. "That's a great idea. But I can't spend the night because I told your dad I'd be home before bedtime. When we're finished eating, I'll check out the spa and see if we can get facials in a couple of hours."

When they finished eating and the trays were taken away, they decided to take a dip in the ocean, knowing it would be cold because of the time of year. Getting in the water was not an easy task. They teased and splashed each other until they were eventually in up to their necks. Nicole loved to swim so it didn't take long before she dove under the water to pick up coral and shells.

"You've always been such a good little swimmer."

"And I have you to thank for that. All the summer days you took me and my friends to the lake." Nicole treaded water and thought about the calories she was burning. "Oh, wait a second." She dived to the bottom and grabbed two handfuls of sand. "We don't need to pay for facials," she said as she gooped the sand on her face and started rubbing it. "See, I'm exfoliating."

Her mom laughed at her. "Get me some."

Nicole dived again and grabbed two more handfuls of sand to give to her mom, then went down for more for herself. They gently scrubbed their faces and laughed at each other for how silly they looked.

Nicole was having the best time with her mother: She didn't feel judged, she'd received many compliments and her mom was sharing her feelings openly about her troubles, not anything to do with men or sex but the deeper issues that helped Nicole think about her own life. Nicole wanted to know who her mom was. And she also wanted to know who *she* was; she didn't want to lose track of herself the way her mother had and Rick's mother had.

Around three, they both went in for massages; it was a nice treat and a great way to wrap up the wonderful day at the beach. Before Nicole's mom dropped her off, she called her dad to let him know that she had a great day and would be home soon. She told Nicole that she liked to check in and let him know what she was up to. Nicole thought it was nice but wondered if they were still working on trust issues. She knew it would take time.

Later that evening, Nicole grabbed a bottle of water from the fridge and picked up a notebook from her desk. She made herself comfortable on the couch, then wrote, *Who is Nicole?* on a blank page. She underlined it. She started with the basics: *Woman, Daughter, Banker.* Then she added, *Friend.*

What makes Nicole happy? What does Nicole like to do? "Hmm." She tapped her pen to her chin. *I like my job. I like my friends. I like my home. I like my parents. I'm starting to like exercising and taking better care of myself. I like that I drink less than I used to. I like Rick. I like reading. I like swimming. I like dancing. I like eating.* She reread what she had written and was a little taken aback realizing that maybe she hadn't done enough to really know what she likes to do. *Maybe I need a hobby? Maybe I should travel?*

The only thing Nicole learned about herself during this little exercise was that she really had a lot more to learn about herself.

Chapter 21

SUNDAY, NICOLE WENT with Renee to a biker event that had been going on all weekend. Renee had done the hair for some of the models, so she had a VIP invite and asked Nicole to join her. At the trade show, Renee pointed out the hair she had done and also who was sleeping with whom. There were booths and venders selling everything from leather clothing, sex toys and jewelry to motorcycles. They walked around talking about relationships and what they meant, why some worked and some didn't. They talked about Nicole's parents, Nicole's failed relationships, Renee's relationship with Jason and Roxanne's new relationship with Mark.

When they walked by a large booth that had panties, bras and negligees, they started searching through a bin of panties. Nicole found a pair. She held them up to herself. They were black with white writing that said, "Well it ain't going to lick itself."

"I love these! I'm getting them."

Renee looked and said, "Oh, my God! I want them!" She snatched them from Nicole.

Then they both started digging in the bin looking for more. Renee found a white pair with black writing and Nicole found another bigger pair in her size, and bought both. She decided she would give the smaller pair in white to Roxanne for a bridal shower gift.

While they were laughing about Roxanne's shock after opening them in front of all her family and friends, Nicole felt a tap on her shoulder. It was Stan.

"Oh, hi, Stan. How are you? How's Carol and Mary or whoever?" Nicole said sarcastically.

He ignored Nicole's question and gave her the same seductive look that made her take him to bed in the first place. Only it didn't work anymore. He looked her up and down and bit his lip.

Nicole wasn't impressed, but Renee was. "Hi, I'm Renee, Nicole's friend and you are?"

"Stan. Nicole and I …"

"We met in the dumpster, Renee. I told you."

"Oh, Stan," she giggled.

"Maybe I should come over later," he said, eyeing her seductively.

"No, no, Stan, you shouldn't."

"Oh, I think I forgot my favorite t-shirt at your house."

"No, I don't think you did."

She grabbed Renee's hand to get away from him.

"Did you keep his t-shirt?"

"No, the dumpster ate it."

"Oh," Renee giggled. "I can see why you went for it. He's gorgeous and that look in his eyes. My God, did you see that look he was giving you?"

They escaped the biker event with new panties and most of their dignity intact. Nicole finally confessed to Renee that she kind of liked a guy from her building. And Renee knew exactly who she was referring to. "I told Roxy that you would end up with him. I knew it. I could see it in his eyes that day at Starbucks. I knew he had big intentions with you."

"But Renee, I don't know what I want. I like him, but I'm not sure I have a spark or that he even has a spark for me."

"Yes, I know. I know all about the spark." She rolled her eyes. "The spark is for sperm. The flame is for long term." She was suddenly all poetic. "You and this condo guy, I'm guessing have the flame."

"Oh, my God, that's the corniest thing I've ever heard. Did you make it up?"

"Yes, I did, a long time ago. Right before I met Jason. We have the flame, and it's forever, baby!"

"Renee, you're not listening to me. I don't know if I want a boyfriend."

"What, you not want a boyfriend? Impossible!"

"No, really. Do I? Do I want a boyfriend?"

Renee leaned toward her and grabbed her arm. "Yes, Nicole, you do want a boyfriend. They are nice to have and if you pick a good guy, a flame, they are good for us."

Nicole felt a lump in her chest and tried to fight the tears. "It's just that I'm… maybe I'm scared."

"We're all a little scared, Nicole. We're just out here doing the best we can. That's all we can do."

Driving home, Nicole genuinely thought about everything Renee had said about relationships, but she just wasn't sure what she wanted. All her life she was taught that she needed somebody to love her, that she needed a man, but now, for the first time in her life, she felt content with herself. She was focusing on her career and health, her family and friends and not on a man. And in some ways the world seemed to be opening up to her. For the first time in her life, she found herself interested more in women than men.

Nicole had never really been afraid of anything when it came to men, but suddenly the possibilities of a real relationship terrified her. She was beginning to realize that all this time she was on this mission to find love, she really just wanted to remain distant and therefore safe from men. She picked losers to avoid a real relationship. She was more interested in the spark and the speed and instant gratification instead of the possibilities of going the distance with somebody, a flame or sharing a future with somebody else.

And what was scaring her was this new concept of women losing themselves in relationships. She couldn't afford to lose something she didn't even have yet. Nicole felt like her whole universe was shifting, her friends were changing, her mom was changing—she was changing.

Chapter 22

WEDNESDAY NIGHT AT seven, Nicole stood at Rick's door with a bottle of wine. He opened the door and kissed her hello.

"Oh, my God! This is your place? It's huge, and beautiful!" Now she understood why some of the doors in the hall were missing numbers because he'd had three condos made into his own. "Wow, I can't believe this! Give me a tour and show me what you did," she said, looking around at the stunning decor. "And I thought I did a lot to mine."

"You did, Nicole. Your place is very nice."

"Well, I have a lot of people to thank for my place."

"So do I. Come on, I'll show you," Rick said, holding her hand as he started the tour. Every time he wanted to point something out, he switched hands with her so he would still be touching her. It made her feel that she was important to him, that he cared about her. He pointed out where the two doors that led to the hall had been. While he didn't think the hall needed changing, he didn't want to see the remnants of the doors in his condo. During the tour, she realized that they had similar taste in decorating.

"Who decorated your place?" Nicole asked, testing to see if an old girl-friend had done it.

"Well, I had help from a couple of guys who have a design center downtown. I told them what I wanted, I showed them pictures from maga-zines and they put it all together. I think they did a great job."

"Yes, it's beautiful." Before Nicole knew what was happening she was pressed against the wall with Rick and his Dick pressing against her. She went weak and couldn't wait to have him.

"You're beautiful," Rick said.

"And you're a tease."

He smiled, holding her hand as they finished the tour in his bedroom. "This is the master bedroom and over here is the master bathroom," he said, leading her into the bathroom. "Well, that's it. Are you hungry?"

"Ah, yeah, but not for food."

Rick laughed. "I'm crazy about you, Nicole," he said, leading her to the kitchen.

"Well, *I've* never been so confused."

"Like I said before, every encounter I've had with you, good or bad, has made me look forward to the next. I still feel that way." He let go of her hand when he showed her where to sit down while he finished making dinner. "I've had my eye on you a lot longer than you realize. I remember when you bought your condo."

"How come I don't remember you?"

"You've been busy," he said, winking at her. "That dumpster was a blessing in some way. That's when you finally saw me."

Nicole smiled, embarrassed. "Sorry."

"That's fine." He smiled confidently. "Timing is everything," he said, "in baseball, business and love."

Suddenly Nicole's flame was burning out of control. Rick was the sexiest man she had ever been lucky enough to be with. And he liked her—he really seemed to like her. This was something entirely new to her. She felt like she had done some dating, and even convinced herself that she dated Rick long enough. Now she wanted some action. "Well, should we eat now or after?"

"Really? Are you ready?"

"I was ready Thursday night. Are you?"

"I was ready a month ago," Rick said and led her back to his bedroom.

Rick started to unbutton Nicole's blouse and Nicole helped Rick take off his shirt. His muscular, hard body took her breath away. Suddenly she felt inferior. But her feelings of inferiority left quickly when he kissed her hard and pressed his hands against her breasts. He touched her in ways she had never been touched before; he touched her as if he knew her body better than she knew her own. She reached for his jeans and started to undo them. She could feel his penis trying to get out. When she started to pull his pants down, Rick grabbed Nicole's wrists and gently pushed her back until she was sitting on his bed. He lifted her arms over her head, and she lay back. He was on top of her pressing against her while holding the small of her back. Dying to feel him inside her, she asked him if he had a condom.

Rick kept caressing her body then moved down to take off her pants. "Are you sure you want to?"

"Yes."

Rick leaned over to his nightstand and got a condom out from an unopened box. Nicole thought she recognized the box as the same one that she and Joy had purchased at the grocery store. She wanted to reach down and feel him, but he sat up to roll on the condom. Nicole tried to get a look but she couldn't tell, because it was too dark. Rick was back on top of her. He kissed her neck and whispered in her ear, "Are you ready?"

Nicole was. Rick gently pressed the tip next to her. He kept caressing her as he slowly and gently slid himself in a little at a time. Nicole knew immediately that he was wearing a large condom. She was going to come, and he wasn't even all the way in. "Oh, my God, I'm going to come."

Rick kept doing what he was doing until he was deep inside her. He started throbbing and pulsating and Nicole could tell he was coming, too. He moaned and they lay there together, still.

"Oh, my God, Nicole. You're so beautiful. Your body's amazing."

Nicole started to cry.

Rick rolled to his side. "Nicole? Oh, no," he said, reaching across her for the lamp and turning it on. "Nicole, did I hurt you?"

"No."

"Are you okay?"

"Yes. I'm…"

He leaned over and kissed her passionately on the lips. "Any regrets?"

She rolled over facing him. "No. You?" She wiped her eyes. "That was amazing."

"You are amazing. No regrets." He gently moved her hair away from her face. "Are you hungry?"

"Yeah, but not for food."

He smiled. "Should we eat now or after?"

"Let's eat. I'd kind of like to watch you make me dinner."

Rick got up and Nicole was able to get a good look at his semi-hard penis and the rest of his body. He was the most beautiful man she had ever seen. His body belonged in magazines modeling underwear. "Rick, your body is incredible."

Rick slipped into a pair of shorts and held his hand out to help Nicole up.

"I'm embarrassed."

"Why? You're beautiful."

Nicole rolled her eyes and held a pillow up to stay covered.

"Here." Rick grabbed one of his t-shirts from his dresser drawer and handed it to her.

She quickly put it on then grabbed his hands for his help to get up. His t-shirt was big on her; it hung down to her mid-thigh. "You're big."

"You're small," he said and motioned for her to lead the way.

Nicole smiled and walked in front of him to the kitchen.

"Can I get you something to drink?" he asked as he stepped behind the counter.

Nicole sat at the bar. His kitchen was much bigger than hers. She could see how he combined the kitchens of two units to create his. "Can I get some water?"

Rick reached into the fridge for two bottles of water. He opened her bottle and handed it to her. "Here you are, Nicole. I have to tell you, I'm having a hard time thinking about food with you in the room. I'm a little distracted."

Nicole smiled. "Is that your way of saying that you want me to help you?"

"No, Nicole. I'm treating you to a spaghetti dinner. My sauce is simmering, and I cheated; I made the pasta shortly before you got here. I'll have to stick it in the microwave for a minute." He stepped over to Nicole and gave her a kiss.

Nicole no longer wanted to eat. Watching Rick in the kitchen made her want to go back to bed. She could watch him and look at him for the rest of her life. The way his muscles looked on his body only made her imagine his muscles working while making love to her.

Rick fixed a plate for Nicole, then for himself. They sat facing each other at the breakfast bar. "Cheers, Nicole." He held up his bottle of water. "To us and our future."

Nicole lifted her bottle to toast. "You think we have a future?"

"So far, so good." He took a bite of his spaghetti. "How about you, what do you think?"

"Well, I enjoy your company and you are extremely sexy and… well… I like you." She took a bite of her bread. "And I want to see how this plays out."

"Well, I'm glad we got the sex out of the way. Now we can just focus on getting to know each other."

"Rick, I think you have that backwards."

Rick smiled and looked Nicole in the eyes. "Nicole, you have the most gorgeous body."

"Rick, why do you keep saying that? I've been overweight my whole life."

"You are not overweight. You are perfect. You are a beautiful, soft woman."

Nicole never heard a compliment like that before. "Thank you."

"Oh, I get it. You compare yourself to the women in magazines."

"And my friends and almost every other woman I've ever met." Nicole laughed. "It's usually my skinny girlfriends telling me that I'm pretty the way I am. Now it's my skinny boyfriend telling me that."

"That sounded nice. Am I your boyfriend?"

"At the moment," she teased.

When they finished eating and cleaning up the kitchen, they made their way back to the bedroom. He begged her to spend the night, but she refused. "I have to go home and let this all sink in. I need some time to sort it all out."

"Is everything okay? I hope you don't regret this."

"No, I don't think I will, but my concern is that we live right next to each other and you pretty much run the joint. What if we don't..."

"Oh, no you don't. You're not going to get all negative on me. Wait until I leave the cover off the toothpaste, or put the roll of toilet paper on wrong, then you can get down on me."

Nicole laughed. "You're right. Okay, deal." She reached her hand out to shake his.

He shook her hand. "Goodnight, Nicole. I'm looking forward to seeing you again. Maybe we should go and see a movie tomorrow, or at least grab a quick lunch."

"That sounds nice." Nicole quickly kissed him goodbye and walked slowly back to her condo. She locked the door and started laughing uncontrollably. She was nervous and happy and giddy.

Nicole lay in bed thinking. Wanting to feel close to Rick, she got up and opened the bedroom blinds, glancing down to look at the dumpster. She could see inside Rick's condo, but she couldn't see him. Nicole still had doubts about this new thing with Rick, but she was willing to see what would happen. She thought about her relationships with men and all the drama that ensued, wondering, hoping that this time she chose one who would stick around, and one that she would want to have stick around. It didn't matter if in her past she felt unworthy or thought the men were unworthy, Nicole hadn't wanted a relationship—until now. And she wouldn't share all the details with her parents or Christian or Blaine or Roxanna or Renee. She would ride this one out on her own.

Nicole was happy. She hadn't felt so at ease and comfortable in her skin before in her life. She still felt nervous about having a new boyfriend, the changes her parents were going though, the changes in her friendships with Renee and Roxanne, and even the idea of losing that nasty dumpster. But that was life and she intended to live it to the fullest. Change was what growing up was all about.

Chapter 23

A FEW DAYS later, Nicole was on Facebook catching up with family and friends when she noticed she had a private message from Kevin, a guy she'd had one date with a couple guys before Tom. But before opening the message, she had to shake off the memory of that horrible evening. She closed her eyes and wondered what was wrong with her. She had flashbacks of sitting in the booth with him, drinking wine and telling him her life story—on their first date!

***

"… and that was the big bodybuilder who was afraid of a three-pound Yorkie. Can you believe it? He was huge, well, not in every way, if you know what I mean, but he was afraid of a tiny, little dog. Then there was Todd, who was sure I had a baby, just because I had stretch marks. Well, I had to break up with him! He was sure I had a kid somewhere. So what? I have stretch marks on my thighs, hips, breasts and a little on my stomach, but that doesn't mean I had a baby. I probably shouldn't say this, but I've struggled with being a little chubby my whole life. I'll get a grip on it some-day." She put her hand up against her stomach. "You should see what hap-pens when I sit for any length of time. I get these red lines across my belly, where my gut creases. Oh, you'll see it later tonight," she said, winking at him.

The server stepped over. "Oh, can I get another glass of wine?" she asked and looked at Kevin. "I guess I won't get a grip on my weight issue tonight," she continued. "I have cellulite, too, all over my legs. I've spent so much money on lotions and treatments to get rid of it, but nothing works." She took another drink of wine. "I'm not an alcoholic, oh, but I've dated my share, well, I'm not sure I'd really call it dating, per say, but…" She laughed mischievously. "I finally had enough when I was going to go on a date with this one guy and he asked me to pick him up at a meeting. So I show up and discover this meeting was an AA meeting, a mandatory, court-ordered AA meeting!" She looked at Kevin. "Can you believe it? And that wasn't the worst. I once had a guy go into seizures because he hadn't had a drink for a few hours. He foamed at the mouth and everything. I had to call 9-1-1 on my date. They took him by ambulance."

Nicole excused herself to go to the bathroom. In the bathroom, she checked herself in the mirror while washing her hands. She was a little taken aback by her appearance. She thought she looked great when she left her place, but suddenly she felt she was beginning to resemble Tammy Faye Baker. She tried to wipe some of her mascara and makeup off under her eyes, but it didn't seem to make a difference. She turned to the vanity to pick up her purse, but it was gone. "Oh, shit!" She stepped back into the stall and checked the back of the door. It wasn't there. "Oh, my God!" She exhaled deeply as she left the bathroom.

When she got back to the table she told Kevin that they had to call the police because somebody had stolen her purse.

He leaned across the table to reach for her bag on her side of the booth and held it up. "Is this it?"

"Oh, my God. Yes. Thank you! You are my life saver." She plopped back down into the booth and continued with the saga of her life. "You know, it hasn't all been fun and games. There've been times when I was really, really hurt, when I'd cry myself to sleep. 'Why won't somebody love me? What is so wrong about me? Please God, send me somebody, anybody. I just want somebody to love me.' I could cry right now thinking about it. Oh, and thank God I can count on only one hand the number of times I thought I was preggers! Preg-gers!" she repeated, only louder and slower, leaning toward him to make sure he heard her. "Did I tell you about my homosexual boyfriends? I secretly want to have sex with them. I mean just because they are gay doesn't mean anything to me, I'm still heterosexual. Ugh! They open their shirts or pull down their pants to show me their well hidden tattoos, and I have to catch my breath. They expose their muscular chests and their tight butts. Mmm-mmm!"

The easier the wine went down, the easier her secret thoughts came up. By the time she was telling him how easy he was to be around and how she finally found a good man, somebody she could be herself with, was right around the time he was ready to go. She told him how thankful she was for their deep, spiritual connection and that she knew they had a bright future together because they had no secrets.

When he finally found a way to get her back into his car to take her home, she told him that she was wearing his favorite color bra and panty set, blue. And she was just drunk enough to undo her shirt and show him. "You wanna know how I know your favorite color?"

"Sure."

"Before our date, I got on Facebook and I read every single post you ever made. It took me hours! But I learned a lot about you, and I now know your favorite color. Blue!" She pulled her shirt open again to show him.

When they got to her condo, he didn't want to come in, though she begged. He said he had to get up early and said goodbye to her in the car. When she got out of the car, she decided to take off her shoes for the walk in, they had been acting funny which caused her to walk funny. As she walked up to her building, he watched her. She tried to look as sexy as she could. When she got inside, she heard him drive off. She knew that because of their amazing connection, they had nothing to prove and that was why he didn't come up with her. They would save that for their next date.

The next morning while she was getting ready for work, she remembered the night before and was mortified. The alcohol had worn off and reality had set in. She wasn't sure if she was still drunk, but she giggled every time she thought about something else she had said on her date with Kevin. "Preggers! I actually said preggers? Oh, my God." She bent over laughing. She knew he would never call her, so she called him—to apologize.

He didn't answer, so she had to leave a message.

"Hi, Kevin, it's Nicole from last night. I'm just calling to apologize for my behavior. I know you must have found me irresistible on our date. I'm sure you're busy ring shopping and talking to your family and friends right now, trying to figure out the right way to ask me to marry you. And you're probably feeling a little rushed, fearing that somebody might swoop in and steal me away from you." She started laughing and continued her message. "Anyway, if you tell anybody how crazy I am, I'll deny it. And I'll make something up about you, that you're a kleptomaniac or something." She became serious. "I just wanted to say I'm sorry, and thanks for being such a great guy."

***

Nicole and Kevin had been secret buddies ever since, usually just on Facebook, but occasionally they'd meet for a cup of coffee and to compare notes on their dating escapades. Nicole opened the Facebook message already knowing what it would say, and she was right. He had met the *one*. Nicole congratulated him and knew their little friendship was over.

She closed her laptop and went to her bedroom to get into her pajamas. She stepped next to her bedroom window and took a good look at the dumpster. For the first time in a long time, she felt like she had nothing to throw away—she didn't have a man to throw away. She was getting comfortable with the idea that she was finally ready to settle down and truly be in a relationship, but she was still scared.

She saw Rick, who she now secretly, endearingly referred to as Rick the *Dick,* in his condo and watched him, smiling contentedly. When he noticed her, she opened the window.

"How are you? How was work?" he asked.

"Great. How about you?"

"I had a great day."

"I was thinking about going for a walk in the morning, you wanna join me?" she asked.

"I'd love to. See you in the morning."

When they closed their windows, Nicole noticed that the back area by the dumpster, had been cleaned up. All the miscellaneous junk and garbage was gone.

Chapter 24

THE NEXT MORNING, Nicole slipped into her tennis shoes just as Rick knocked on the door. Nicole was quiet on their fast-paced walk, and at times had to jog a little to keep up with Rick. He was in such great shape, and she was jiggling where she knew she shouldn't be jiggling. She was thankful Rick was beside her and not behind her watching the shifting waves throughout her body. She wondered if the other women walking and jogging on that path had problems with cellulite, too. Fretting inwardly about her shortcomings, she watched a man zoom past them riding a skateboard. He was wearing large gloves, the size of boxing gloves, to push himself along the path because he had no legs.

In that moment, Nicole's negativity about her body changed. She looked up at the sky and thought, *Okay, I get it.* She thought about that saying, *I felt bad I had no shoes until I met a man who had no feet.* She had to quit feeling sorry for herself. If she didn't like being overweight, she had to change it. If she didn't want to change it, she needed to shut up about it and quit whining. The man on the skateboard wasn't whining.

After about a mile, they came to a cute little café and Rick asked if they could stop for a glass of lemonade. "This place has the best lemonade," he said. So while he was inside getting their drinks, Nicole sat at a little bistro table outside watching the foot traffic and cars rush by. The server brought out their lemonade, and Nicole realized that Rick must have gone to the bathroom. *Was that why he had been so quiet?* She started laughing. *Or maybe it just came on him suddenly and he had to make an excuse to stop.* She took a sip of the lemonade, *It's not that good. Maybe he's just going number one, but it's taking some time.* She nervously laughed again. *What if he's sick with the flu? I guess I could hail a cab and get him home.* She sipped her lemonade and waited.

She watched an old man on a bicycle approaching the intersection. He wasn't paying attention and his front tire went into a grate, flipping him over his bike. Nicole jumped up and ran over to him, along with another man who was jogging.

"Oh, my God! Are you okay?"

His arm was scrapped up and the side of his leg had hit the curb. His injuries looked more like a rug burns, with little bleeding from them.

"I'm fine," he barked, then started complaining about his wife. "She said I needed to exercise. She wanted me to go for a bike ride. 'We're only a block from the path,' she said. Now look at me! She thinks exercise is healthy. Yeah, like this is going to save my life. I was safer sitting in my easy chair with the remote watching basketball. God damn it! If I broke my hip…" He tried to get up but couldn't so the jogger called for an ambulance.

"Just stay where you are. You don't want to hurt yourself worse. Let the EMTs check you out, okay?" Nicole said.

"You're kind of cute. What are you, a nurse?"

"No, I'm Nicole. What's your name?"

"Ernest."

"Ernest, can we call your wife for you?"

"God damn it! Now she's going to worry about me."

Rick stepped up just as the ambulance arrived. He stayed out of it and watched Nicole get Ernest's phone number to call his wife. There was no answer. The EMTs decided to take him to the hospital, so Nicole chose to go along to help. "I'm sorry, Rick, but I'm going to stay with Ernest until we get a hold of his wife or kids."

Nicole hopped in the back of the ambulance and held Ernest's hand. "Ernest, your wife isn't home. Is there somebody else I can call?"

"My wife passed away last year." He squeezed Nicole's hand. "I miss her," he said and a tear ran across his temple. "I just don't want people thinking I'm a lonely old man. My granddaughter and her husband live close by. You can call them."

The EMT handed her a phone to use. Ernest's granddaughter was distraught and asked to talk to him. "God damn it, Heather. You don't need to worry about me! I'm fine! No, I am not going to live with you... Oh! ...my heart!"

The EMT jumped toward him and Ernest shook his head no and slapped the EMT away from him. He winked at Nicole.

"Stress! Stress!" he said, hanging up on Heather. "She said she'd meet us at the hospital."

"You're awful!" Nicole said, as she took the phone from him.

"She worries about me too much. She wants me to live with them, but they have their own life, it's new and fresh. I can't stand these old people who expect their kids to stop living to take care of them. I had my life, and I lived a great life. I'm not going to be responsible for taking something away from these young kids who are just starting out. I'm still capable of taking care of myself. Heather's already dealt with too much. My daughter ran off when Heather was twelve. We've taken care of her, her grandmother and I. My wife always wanted more kids and never did like Heather's mom. We call her Heather's mom, we don't even use her name. So it just worked out."

Nicole, chuckling to herself, said, "Sounds like you just take life as it comes. Can you teach me how to do that?"

"Sure," he said, rolling to his side to share his secret with Nicole. He motioned for her to lean in closer. Then very loudly, he said, "Just take life as it comes." He nodded his head confidently, as if he had just shared with her the most important information of her life. Then, exhausted from sharing that important message, he lay back again.

The EMT chuckled, so Nicole gave him a dirty look, then reached for Ernest's hand again. "I think I'm in love with you," she said.

He smiled and covered her hand with his other hand.

By the time Nicole left the hospital by cab, she had all Heather's phone numbers and Ernest's home number. He refused to own a cell phone. He was afraid, at age eighty-seven, that he might get brain tumors. Nicole also learned all about Ernest's small family and how they were probably as troubled as her own. It was clear that Heather was raised by her grandfather. She was just as feisty as he was and they fed off each other.

With every "God damn it!" from Ernest, came a "Don't use the name of the Lord in vain" from Heather.

Ernest walked out of the hospital with a small fracture in his femur, pain medication and a cane. He was to stay off his leg as much as possible and agreed to stay with Heather until he was better able to get around on his own. Nicole was relieved he would be taken care of but did volunteer her time, purposely saying she'd babysit if Heather needed a break.

Nicole was crazy about these people. She felt like she was in the middle of a reality TV show and she couldn't wait to see what would happen next.

Chapter 25

THE NEXT MORNING, Nicole was feeling great. She had a new friend and a new grandpa. She had been thinking about her grandpa a lot lately, and Ernest just stirred up more memories of him. She missed him, even his gentle craziness.

After seeing the legless man on his skateboard and Ernest's willingness to ride his bicycle, Nicole was more inspired than ever to walk and exercise, so she took off on another morning walk. She saw Rick crossing the street.

"How's Ernest?"

"He's great. Small fracture in his thigh." Nicole started laughing. "I haven't talked to you since you had your big dump," she teased, "and you missed all the action. Maybe we should have dinner tonight so I can fill you in?"

"Really? Because I was thinking that maybe I could fill *you* in. But now, suddenly, I'm not feeling that sexy," he said and grinned back at her.

Nicole threw her arms around him. "You're the one who wanted to speed things up. I'm just trying to keep up," she said, with her heart fluttering at the idea of him filling her in. It had been a few days since they made love. "And, yes, I'd like you to fill me in."

He leaned in to kiss her. "What time?"

"Seven." Nicole decided to go in a different direction than usual on her walk and found herself close to a golf course. She wondered if she would like golf. As she was getting ready to cross the street, a golf ball went zipping past her head then bounced a few yards behind her. She ducked and ran for cover, then turned and walked back in the other direction, away from the golf course. She hadn't realized how dangerous it was. She didn't think she'd like golf.

Her phone rang and it was Roxanne wanting to borrow a pair of her shoes. Because of Ernest, Nicole vowed to never walk without her cell phone again. There were often older people walking around and sometimes the walking paths were close to busy roads. With her phone clipped to her hip, she felt safer and better able to help anyone else who might be in trouble.

The rest of the walk Nicole spent imagining her sex date with Rick that evening. She didn't understand why she hadn't used that feature of her building more frequently. It was, after all, very convenient.

When Nicole got home with a vanilla latte, she went straight into her bedroom to lay out the clothes she would wear over to Rick's. Not that it really mattered, but she at least wanted to wear a pretty bra and panties. Thinking of Kevin finding love, she giggled and chose the blue set she had worn on her infamous date with Kevin. She looked out at Rick's window to see if he was in sight, but he wasn't. That's when she noticed that it looked like some type of fence was going up behind the dumpster.

***

After their first round of wild, crazy sex, Rick and Nicole were in his kitchen getting a drink. Nicole chose a Diet Coke, and Rick kept taking sips from her can.

"So, Nicole, I think you've lost a few pounds. You look great."

"Really? Thank you," she said. "You're right, I've lost eight pounds." She sat down on his bar stool while he searched for something in the refrigerator. "I've enjoyed my walks, but I think Ernest is right; exercise can be dangerous." She told him about the golf ball whipping past her head. "I mean, if that thing would have hit me…"

"You know, Nicole, you're probably right. Exercise is dangerous and can be risky. You, for example, might consider walking the path an extreme sport, the way some think skiing snow-covered mountain peaks, outrunning avalanches or surfing the most dangerous waves are extreme. The stationary bike, another fine example, can be quite the challenge. I mean, come on, let's face it, you could fall off."

Nicole glared at him. "You've been dying to say that to me, planning, probably even rehearsing, just waiting for the right opportunity. You think you're soooo funny."

Rick stood there, smiling proudly and nodding his head. "I do think it's funny."

"Well, I guess you're right. It's extreme enough for me to start carrying my phone. Anything could happen out there!"

Rick stepped between Nicole's legs and she wrapped her legs around him. He leaned down and gave her a tender kiss. "I am so glad I met you. I'm crazy about you."

"I'm glad I met you, too." She squeezed her legs around him a little tighter. "Will you take me golfing? I want to know if I would like golfing."

Rick got a little excited. "I'd love to. And I think you'll like it."

She smiled at him proudly, excited to try something new with Rick. She also thought it would be good for her career; other bankers and many of her clients enjoyed a good game of golf.

Chapter 26

NICOLE'S DAD CALLED a few days later. "Hi, honey. We'd really like to see you before we go."

"Go where? What are you talking about?"

"Oh, yeah, your mother and I are going on a cruise for a month."

"A month?"

"Yes, honey, so we would like to see you before we go."

"Of course, Daddy. But why a whole month?" Nicole felt a deep ache in her chest. Even though she didn't see her parents often, still they were always there. And she was starting to feel closer to her mom than she had in years.

"When are you leaving?"

"Six days."

"Six days?" *Oh, my God. I need to sit down.* She took a deep breath and exhaled slowly as her mouth puckered. "Well, I'm really happy for you. How exciting! Where are you going?"

"Okay, baby, I'll be right there," her dad yelled. "Your mother's calling... she's... well... she's ready for me."

Dazed by the thought of her parents making love, Nicole shook her head as if trying to make the thought go away.

"Oh honey, we thought we could come and stay the night with you, leave our car at your place, and then you could take us to the ship in Miami. We have to be there by four the next afternoon. How does that sound? We'll go out for a nice dinner. You pick the place. Oh, I've started an exercise program your mother has me on, and I've already lost five pounds. I'm feeling better than I have in years!" her dad said. "Coming! Honey, I gotta go. Your mother... well, you know." And he hung up the phone.

Nicole put the phone down and fell back onto the couch. *A whole month.* She felt those familiar feelings of fear and nervousness about her parents leaving for so long. *Grow up, Nicole. They deserve this trip. Be happy for them.* She talked herself through her worries and the discomfort changed to excitement for her parents, even though she was still uneasy about them being away for so long.

She heard a knock at the door and was suddenly pissed that Rick lived so close. She didn't want a pop-in type of relationship. She didn't pop in on him. She pulled herself off the couch getting ready for their first fight, she opened her door and it was Tom who stood there. At first, she was thrilled and gave him a huge smile; then just as quickly, her face metamorphosed into an angry scowl.

"What are you doing here?" Nicole asked angrily.

"I was hoping we could talk."

"About what? How easy I am?"

"Well," Tom said, smiling. "Listen, I'm sorry. You look great. I saw you at the bank the other day, and now I can't stop thinking about you."

"Well, I guess you'll have to try harder, because I *haven't* been thinking about you!"

"Come on," he said, stepping closer to her. "Don't be so stubborn. Let me in so we can talk."

"Please! That's pathetic! You blew it. You know the saying, something about you don't know what you've got till it's gone. You've heard of it, haven't you? Well, sorry, it's gone!"

"Come on, Nicole."

"Even if I didn't have a boyfriend, I wouldn't let you in. For me, it's kind of like that old saying, maybe you've heard of it, you don't know what you got till it's gone." She smiled triumphantly. "Well, it works both ways, and I'm lucky you're gone."

"You're really not going to let me in?"

"I guess you missed the part about having a boyfriend." Nicole glanced to the right and saw Rick striding toward her, with his shirt off and hanging over his shoulder. He scooped her up and pressed his amazing body against hers, backing her right into her condo and closing the door behind them.

Nicole and Rick quietly laughed behind the door, and Rick said, "I'm sorry. I've always wanted to do something like that and I figured this was my only opportunity. I loved the way you said you had a boyfriend."

Nicole was still laughing as she said, "You should have seen the look on his face."

"You should have seen the look on yours."

"Rick, you are kind of a dork. You know that, right?"

"Well, I'm not so sure about that." He pressed her against the door and held her arms over her head, pressing himself against her, and continuing to kiss her. He lifted her skirt and pulled her panties to the side, and kneeling, buried his face between her legs.

Nicole was suddenly a fan of oral.

By the time they finished making love, they were in her bed naked. Nicole needed to talk. "I know we all love to hear these four words," she said, ruefully, "but, we need to talk."

"All right," he said, turning on his side and facing her with a sheepish grin. "Let's have it."

"Why are you so confident?"

"It's not that, Nicole. I just like to hear you talk."

She tried not to laugh. "Okay, here's the problem. I'm afraid this is just going to be about sex."

"It certainly isn't for me. Is it for you?"

"I'm not sure. I just don't know if I like you enough to go the distance."

"Hmm?" He looked up, then back to Nicole.

"I really haven't told my friends or my parents about you, and I'm not sure why."

"Well, maybe we should have a few dates and slow down on the sex."

"Yeah, maybe. I guess I'm afraid if I tell somebody, I'll jinx it."

"Maybe we should test it."

"I guess we could do that." She reached for her phone and dialed Renee's cell with Rick's hand resting on her upper thigh.

"Hi, Renee." It was her voicemail. "I'm just calling to tell you that I, well, I guess I have a boyfriend. His name is Rick and I'm not really sure about anything right now, so you can't meet him, and I don't want you fantasizing about him sexually, okay?" Nicole hung up the phone and turned back to Rick.

"What the hell was that?" he said and started to laugh.

Nicole laughed, too. "My friend," she affectionately said, "one of my best friends."

Chapter 27

NICOLE HAD TO meet her parents at the restaurant because they were getting into town later than expected, and Nicole wanted to bring a date. She knew her parents would love him as much as she did. She and Ernest got to the restaurant before her parents so they could catch up on the latest with each other and their families. Like school kids, they sat at the table giggling and gossiping while they waited for Nicole's parents.

"God damn it, Heather fusses over me worse than her grandmother did," Ernest grumbled.

"Maybe because she loves you and she wants to," Nicole said, leaning toward Ernest. "Did you ever think of that?"

Ernest squeezed her hand, saying, "You are just as feisty as all the women I've ever had in my life. What? Am I cursed?"

Nicole laughed. "You love women, that's your problem. The feistier, the better." She squeezed his hand back. "And women can smell that on you, and we love you for it."

Ernest looked over just as Nicole's parents were stepping up to the table. Because of her last conversation with her dad, Nicole was worried that they would not be able to keep their hands off each other in public. But surprisingly, they did not embarrass her as she had expected them to. They were affectionate and considerate with each other. As always, her father helped her mother with her chair and to find a place to set her purse, but clearly there were changes happening in their relationship and Nicole liked what she saw. She reached across the table for her mother's hand, squeezing it and smiling up at her. Nicole felt they shared a new bond.

They were a little surprised to see Nicole's date, and Ernest picked up on it. "Honey, should we tell them now about our plans to marry?" he said straight-faced and shaky.

Nicole's Diet Coke came shooting out of her nose, spilling onto her plate and the tablecloth in front of her. Her mother stood up quickly, disgusted and not wanting to get it on her new blouse. Then just as quickly as if wanting to avoid perfection, she sat back down and laughed with the rest of them.

"Ouch!" Nicole said, laughing and holding the napkin to her face. "It burns. Make it stop!" She couldn't stop laughing.

Ernest called a waiter over to clean up the mess. "There, we're even," he said, handing her plate to the waiter.

"Mom, Dad, this is Ernest, my friend. I met him while he was trying to kill himself on, well, off the bike path." She turned to look at him. "I guess you could say, I'm his hero. I saved him that day from hurting himself worse. Right, Ernest?"

"Very nice to meet you," her mother said. "And if you're going to marry our daughter…"

"We need to tell you all about her," her father interrupted, winking at Nicole.

The evening proceeded with funny, heartwarming stories and memories about each other's families. Later on, Nicole confessed to her parents that she really did have a boyfriend and that she had texted him to join them for coffee after dinner. "He should be here any minute."

"Yeah, but I'm not sure he's right for her. He was in the shitter while Nicole was saving my life," Ernest teased.

"Ernest," she said, giggling, "that's private!"

Everybody laughed.

Just then, Rick walked up to the table and everybody but Ernest stood up to great him. Nicole introduced him to her father first, and then to her mother, Elisabeth. "This is my boyfriend, Rick."

Rick gave Nicole a quick kiss on the cheek, then reached over to shake hands with Ernest. "Hey, buddy. How's it going?"

They scooted over to make room for Rick, and ordered coffee for everyone and a couple of deserts to share. The conversation flowed easily as if they had all known each other for years. Nicole was happy and crazy in love. Rick fit right into her family—into her life.

She loved her parents and seeing them treating each other so kindly made Nicole choke up a little. She'd really missed them and was thankful to have them back together, better than ever. She loved being around Ernest, and she had been right about her parents liking him. They adored Ernest, and even invited him to come and stay with them when they returned from their trip. To Nicole's surprise, he said he'd love to. She couldn't help but feel like they had Grandpa back—her family was complete once again.

Chapter 28

ABOUT A WEEK after her parents left on the cruise, Nicole got home late from work. She'd been frazzled all day because she didn't sleep the night before, and she'd pushed snooze too many times on her alarm clock this morning. She'd had a rough day and was so looking forward to the weekend.

Glancing out her bedroom window before getting into her pajamas, she froze and turned back for another look. "Oh, my God!" she sobbed, holding her hand to her heart and staring in disbelief at the space where her dumpster had once been. She opened the window for a better look.

The area was fenced with an elegant, white, decorative enclosure. The muddy ground was now covered with natural-stone pavers, and potted plants and flowers placed around the site. Four natural-stone benches, one on each side, faced the center of the area where a large stone fountain gurgled invitingly.

Nicole couldn't believe her eyes. It was the most beautiful little garden she had ever seen. "How can this be?" she murmured, certain that the dumpster had been there in the morning when she'd gone to work.

The soothing sounds of the water made her dream. She closed her eyes and imagined she was by a river with a waterfall in Minnesota without a care in the world. She felt like she was sixteen again, or thirteen or eight when she was naive and innocent. She breathed in the fresh Cannon River and the clean Minnesota air with not a trace of garbage in it. She didn't want to open her eyes and find that it was only a dream.

Tapping on the window brought her back to reality. It was Rick, who waved and smiled at her. She waved and smiled back. When he lifted his window, Nicole could barely speak. "It's beautiful," she whispered, her throat and chest tightening, and again she held her hand to her heart as tears flooded her eyes. She tried to say more but couldn't. She just kept crying and holding her hand over her heart.

"Go down and take a look. Try out the benches," he said. "Oh, and Nicole, I love you."

It was the best day of her life. "I love you, too," she said.

She left her window open and walked downstairs to make sure it was real. Stepping off the last step, she realized she was already in the garden. The only gate led from the garden into the alley. The sandstone felt wonderful on her bare feet. And the smell, she couldn't get over the fragrance in the air from the flowers. She sat down on a bench facing the fountain. She just couldn't believe it. How could this be? She closed her eyes again, listening to the splashing of the fountain and smelling the flowers. And the tears kept coming. Her emotions were out of control.

It felt like Rick created the garden and designed it especially for her. Every detail symbolized something important in her life. The fence would protect her and control who and when somebody was a part of her life. The fountain mimicked the joyful dancing of her happy heart. The pavers kept her grounded and buried past mistakes. The benches, facing all four directions, allowed her to look at things from every angle. And the flowers were colorful like her and all the beautiful people in her life.

Nicole trailed her hand in the fountain. Then she walked around the garden slowly turning in a circle. She closed her eyes and opened her arms, and her fear flew away—she wasn't afraid of the future. She wasn't afraid of change. She wasn't lonely or alone. Nicole felt beautiful and happy and she was looking forward to growing old with Rick and all her family and friends.

She knew Rick was the one.

Author Becky Due

Becky Due is the new voice of women's fiction. She has the courage, honesty and writing style for today's busy women, and she does not cringe away from hard issues. She will leave you feeling strong, self-confident, independent, and in control of your life.

Her books have won and been finalists in several independent competitions including the 2010 and 2011 National Indie Excellence Awards, USA Book News and the 2009 IPPY Awards.

Other Great Titles by Becky Due

The Gentlemen's Club: A Story for All Women (Novel)

Touchable Love: An Untraditional Love Story (Novel)

Returning Injury: A Suspense Celebrating Women's Strength (Novel)

The Dumpster: One Woman's Search for Love (Novel)

Traveling for Love: Searching for Self, Hoping for Love (Novel)

Blue the Bird: On Flying (Children's)

The Woman's Handbook: Everything You Want To Say To Your Daughter, Sister, Niece, Friend In One Simple Book (Gift Book/Self-Help)

2 Days to Healthy Self-Esteem (Self-Help)

I'm Upset! App for Women (App)

Visit Becky Due at

www.BeckyDue.com
http://www.facebook.com/BeckyDue.Author
www.twitter.com/BeckyDue

www.ingramcontent.com/pod-product-compliance
Lightning Source LLC
Chambersburg PA
CBHW050823180626
46814CB00004B/1437